A Paler Shade of Blue

MICHAEL ETTINGER

First published in paperback by
Michael Terence Publishing in 2023
www.mtp.agency

Copyright © 2023 Michael Ettinger

Michael Ettinger has asserted the right to be identified as the
author of this work in accordance with the
Copyright, Designs and Patents Act 1988

ISBN 9781800945128

The concepts expressed, and the thoughts are of the Author alone.
The places and the people portrayed including
their names and the events described in these notes
have no resemblance to any actual event or
person living or dead, other than those people
who by their work and publications
are in the public domain

No part of this publication may be reproduced, stored in
a retrieval system, or transmitted, in any form or by
any means, electronic, mechanical, photocopying,
recording or otherwise, without the prior
permission of the Author

Cover image
Oleg Dudko
Copyright © www.123rf.com

Cover design
Copyright © Michael Terence Publishing

For my good friend, Brian Wynn.

Chapter 1
21st December 2015

I remember Rebecca or to be more precise, I'll never forget her. We first met at Charlie Patterson's Christmas bash he holds every year at Claridge's, an exclusive five-start hotel in Mayfair.

Charles George Patterson to give him his full title is the chairman of Berkshire Developments based in Brook Street, Mayfair and each year he holds a charity dinner and auction on behalf of 'Save the Children'.

Guests mainly wealthy businessmen and their wives are expected to both donate and bid for the lots which this time included a nineteen ninety five Jaguar XJ6, a number of small paintings by Monet, Kandinsky, Warhol and Cezanne. There was a collection of valuable watches and jewellery, plenty to go at after the food. I must point out that I don't belong to the wealthy set, I guess I'm reasonably well off if you include my three bed roomed flat in St Johns Wood, and working as an architect for the people on the top table, I live day to day with a small overdraft from the local bank. Charlie, as he liked to be called by his inner circle of business associates and close friends, made it clear he expected the auction festivities to raise over three million pounds, this time, deep pockets required all round. Each guest had already paid six hundred pounds for their place at a table. A tidy sum for 'Save the children', before a bite of food or a glass of bubbly was consumed.

The three hundred guests were seated around thirty tables, fanned out in the shape of a semi circle, table 1 being the top table, then three tables, four tables, six tables, seven tables and nine tables. I found I was on the sixth row, two up from last year when I was at the rear, on the ninth row, so I must be doing something right. Guests began to arrive at four thirty and dinner was served at five o'clock, by around six o'clock immediately after dinner was complete the auction commenced usually lasting four hours, what wasn't sold was taken by Ruben Goldstein and sold through his antiques shop in Holborn and the money raised given to Charlie during the coming year. It was a long evening for some, many consumed too much to drink, and others engaged in networking, others both male and female were on the look out for clandestine adventure. Nobody without good reason left until Charlie pronounced the auction over. The way Charlie saw it, Berkshire Developments turnover was five Billion of which three and a half Billion was paid out mainly to the companies represented around the tables, a slap up meal and an auction was not too much to ask, to Charles Patterson's way of thinking, it was a way of giving back. I was seated next to Pamela Stephenson to my left, she had a kind face, attractive, smartly dressed, fiftyish, old money, the wife of John Stephenson a well heeled big wheel in highway infrastructure and to my right was Edith Wharton, who looked a bit of a tom boy or a little man, with her close cropped mousy brown hair parted to one side, pinstriped grey suit, white shirt and dark blue tie, I guessed early forties, she was an associate of Carters, the high flyers of the commercial building, insurance industry, forget what she looked like, she was considered in the city as a mover and shaker. In all probability Edith earned more in a week than I earned in a year. Since Jane my wife died six years ago from breast cancer, I rarely socialised, when I did which wasn't often, I went out alone. Prior to her becoming ill, in the five years of our marriage we had a great life together, Jane had worked for a publishing Company and I had set up in practice as an Architect.

We had a good social life and enjoyed what other people might describe as the trappings of success; I was thirty seven, six feet two in my socks, coming up fifteen stone with a fine head of brown hair, some kind people said I was reasonably good looking in a rugged sort of way but not what you would call handsome. Neither was I vain but in those days I liked to dress well and looked the part of a successful businessman enjoying life. Since Jane's untimely death aged thirty four, I had lost over two stone or more in weight, my dark brown hair was peppered with grey and whilst I didn't look scruffy I looked gaunt. I hadn't bought any new clothes except for shoes for the past five years, it wasn't that I was still grieving, which I supposed in some ways I still was, but I had no reason to buy any, apart from work, I didn't go anywhere. If the clothes were a little loose on me I didn't notice, my friends, the few I still had either understood my grief and gave me the space to mourn in my own way or were too polite to say let it go, you're too young to mope. It had been difficult at first, there were no children to look after or comfort but I forced myself to continue my work, which was the only form of meeting people and enjoyment I had, though in the past year, I was getting back to a little like my old self. I had put on a few pounds and my clothes were beginning to fit me again. I had bought a new dress shirt for the Christmas do, and a new black bow tie, a proper one this time, which you tied at the back rather than an adjustable band, it took me about half an hour on a good day, today was one of them and I had my eyes on the XJ6 Jag that was in the auction. I was getting there, wherever there was but it was a slow and sometimes painful business. I wasn't prepared for the changes and events which were to usher in the New Year, but then again neither was I prepared for the changes that I had to endure, following Jane's untimely death. Change it seems is part of life's rich pattern, no matter how much we resist and try to keep things on an even keel, change is waiting in the shadows, ready to pounce, mainly when you are not looking. This though was a function I dare not miss if I wanted to remain in business as an Architect working indirectly for Berkshire Developments. It didn't matter to Charlie Patterson how good you were, attendance at his charity function when invited was mandatory, as was bringing an item for the auction and buying something at an outrageous price if you wanted to be part of the Berkshire merry-go-round. His loyal accountant Jim Housegood would be seated next to Charlie, Jim was a gaunt, mousy looking thin man with grey hair, balding on top, his DJ had seen better days and he had the look of someone who had lost a lot of money. Jim rarely smiled unless it involved money coming his way but he was a very able accountant, together he and Charlie would keep tabs on who brought and who bought what. He was known in the city as 'Crafty Jim', he lived the frugal life but was a millionaire many times over. Woe betide the skin flint, this was not the place to be. Over the year I had spent sometime searching for something which was valuable but wouldn't cost me a fortune. I was lucky enough to be given a small painting by Kandinsky in settlement of an outstanding debt, when one of my clients Mary Potter, a widow, found herself unable to pay my fees for a retail refurbishment in Cork Street, when the bank pulled the plug. At the time said I did not mind waiting until things improved for her but Mary insisted I take the painting. I rather like Kandinsky's work but this was a worthy cause and saved me from extending my overdraft.

Next to Pamela Stephenson to my left was Walter Smith a rather fat and bloated structural engineer who thought he was the incarnation of Islamabad Kingdom Brunel the famous Civil and Structural Engineer of the nineteenth century. At social functions such as these, Walter was a crushing bore and was one of the few men not wearing a DJ. Instead he wore a pale blue shirt, green kipper tie and a light grey suit, the jacket hung open due to his size, the tie came down to the third button of his shirt, his pink podgy fingers were wrapped around the stem of a glass filled to the brim with red wine, it was only a matter of time before the green kipper tie would have a red pattern on it to give both Walter and the tie an abstract appearance. I felt sorry for Pamela and the woman seated the other side of Walter, whom I did not know, they were in for a night of Engineering, ear bashing. Walter would go into minute detail of steel beams, shapes and sizes, stress points and weak foundations, cantilevers and spans, never tired of telling his audience, how complex structural engineering was and how he alone solved the most complex of structural problems. The woman unknown to me appeared the exact opposite of Walter Smith, where he was fat and rather ugly the woman who when later was introduced to me, was Rebecca Davis, she was slim, attractive rather than pretty. She had a way of smiling, speaking and mannerisms which only come with breeding. I figured she was in her late thirties or early forties, in any event she commanded attention from the other guests around the table, she had my vote not that it was a contest. Her hair was a soft brown, cut around the shape of her oval face and elegant neck, to reveal pearl earrings. I couldn't quite make out the colour of her eyes I was too far away, they looked dark brown, alert and bright, her skin was flawless, and no make-up other than a soft red lip stick applied to her bow shaped lips. She wore a dark blue dress, cut short at the shoulder; a string of pearls gave light and grace to her overall appearance. I was inclined to think she knew she was attractive, but not overly bothered if those around the table didn't share the same view. She had more strings to her bow than good looks and fine clothes. I guessed she was both clever and intelligent a rare combination male or female. I noticed she didn't wear a ring on either hand, as I took a sip of my first glass of wine of the evening. I refused to accept that Rebecca not wearing a wedding ring was somehow important to me, it's not something I would normally notice or dwell on but I admit I was intrigued and hoped to get to know her better during the course of the evening. Rebecca listened politely to Walter banging on about how he had single handed remodelled the new shopping centre in the West Midlands, to account for weak foundations and a damaged bridge which was near by and flood plane issues over the first course of the dinner. Rebecca gave me a knowing look that suggested boredom. When she tried to change the subject by asking Walter had he been on holiday this year? He answered by waving his short fat arms in the air with an intensity of a scalded cat, saying that he had no time for holidays, he ran a tight ship and enjoyed being hands on. He mentioned that that was a lie, he had taken his wife Deirdre to St Ives for an over night stay for a conference on structural sea defences, wouldn't do it again he said, too much driving and it rained both days. The waiter, Manuel, passed by and Walter asked for a refill of red wine.

"Up to the top if you don't mind," he said, his words slightly slurred. As much as I was intrigued by the presence of Rebecca, I spent my time exchanging pleasantries with Edith who also was very interesting, I wanted to avoid getting collared by Walter at any cost, I had been caught a couple of times at functions we had both attended, his rumbling monologue was a fate worse than death. Things brightened up in a curious way, over the main course we were treated to learning that Walter had bought a Clarice Cliff tea pot at a car boot sale for thirty five pounds which was lot twenty nine in the auction. He said he expected it might reach two hundred pounds despite the small chip in the spout. I think we all suppressed a laugh. Walter had that pompous manner of Sidney Green Street, he was so busy talking he did not notice that he had missed his mouth with the fork and a piece of potato and a slice of roast beef lodged between his shirt and tie. We all stopped eating and watched spell bound waiting for the items of food to fall into his lap, as it happened he noticed before they fell and with his desert spoon scooped the offending food up with a practiced flourish and pushed them into his mouth, then furiously began rubbing his tie with the napkin. When he had finished and began to talk to Rebecca, she stopped him in his tracks.

"You've missed a bit Walter."

"Oh, really," he replied. His face the colour of beetroot, he began looking about himself, nearly knocking his wine over as he searched his apparel.

"On your chin Walter."

He began rubbing the right side of his face with the napkin.

"Other side, Walter."

He rubbed the left side of his chin and the offending piece of mash potato flew off his chin landing on the table beside Pamela's side plate, which he scooped up with a butter knife and popped into his mouth. I was beginning to feel it had been worth coming, entertainment as well as a meal. After apologising profusely to Pamela Walter soon got back on track, asking her if she knew how long it took to repaint the golden gate bridge in San Francisco? No she didn't know, she said as she got up to go to the powder room. Of course Walter Smith was a very good Engineer, if he wasn't he would not have been here. He was to be seen at his best, standing in a trench, wearing wellies, hard hat, vis vest, up to his ankles in mud deciding how deep the foundations should be. He had saved Berkshire Developments a huge sum of money by designing a pile and raft construction over some dodgy ground at a new Shopping Centre in Walsall. It was all about handling him Charlie would say to those who had received a Walter ear bashing.

"When Walter gets his engineering high horse out and begins chomping at the bit, you just need to say in a stern but polite voice, we don't need the high horse today Walter." Going on to say Walter would usually take the hint and shut up; we laughed at the time, it was a pity Charlie was not on our table. The excitement grew as the meal came to its conclusion and the steady consumption of alcohol began to take effect on most of us. Charlie got up and addressed his guests, introducing Bill Granger the auctioneer and Suzy Spencer his scantily dressed assistant to roars of approval from the male guests. The first lot was a Victorian diamond broach, given by Bernard Rutherford's wife. Bernard was the MD of Carter's. To show what was expected, Charlie made an opening bid of fifty K. There were a number of bids from the top three tables with the broach being knocked down to Charlie for ninety K, he looked pleased with himself, his bird like eyes, darting around the room to see that everyone knew what was expected. The pace was fast and furious; the Monet went for four hundred K just three bids, the Cezanne after a slow start also went for four hundred and fifty, the Warhol silk screen print of Chairman Mau went for two hundred and ninety K and my small Kandinsky, fetched a tidy forty five K, which would have gone some way to my buying the Jag and some. I tried not to think about that. We had another laugh on our table when Walter's tea pot came up for sale. At first there were no bids then glaring at Walter, Charlie made a bid of four hundred pounds, knowing what was expected of him, Walter raised his hand and the price went to six hundred pounds, a further bid came from Charlie taking the tea pot to eight hundred pounds before being knocked down to Walter for one thousand pounds. Suzy the auctioneer's assistant brought the Claris Cliff tea pot over to Walter, wriggling her backside like a well known Hollywood actress, purring his name like he was the president of the United States she planted a wet kiss on his bald head and handed him the tea pot.

Normally Walter would have enjoyed being kissed on the head by Suzy but his red face was bursting with anger; he had just paid one thousand pounds plus the original purchase price of thirty five pounds for a worthless tea pot with a damaged spout. He looked at his fellow guests around the table and forced himself to say,

"Well it's for a good cause."

Next up were some blue diamond ear rings set in platinum. There was a moment of silence before Bill asked for an opening bid. A hand went up from the top table but I couldn't see who it was, other than a mans hand.

"Five thousand pounds," he said. This was followed by a bid of ten thousand pounds and so it went up to Eighty thousand pounds when Rebecca raised her hand.

"Ninety thousand, new bidder," Bill said. There was another moment of silence before Bill asked for any more bids and after a further moment he banged down his gavel.

"Table three Suzy."

Suzy walked over as before wriggling her backside as she came up to Rebecca.

"Here you are Rebecca, aren't they are beautiful, you lucky girl," Suzy said, handing her a small platinum and satin cushioned box. If Suzy was pretending to be Marylyn Monroe then Rebecca reminded me of Jean Simmons. We all stared at Rebecca who simply smiled and put the box in a small black leather clasp bag.

"I think yours is up next David," she said smiling. She was looking directly at me as Bill gave his spiel about the XJ6. It was true; I was interested in the Jag but expected it to be out of my price range. Charlie got up and said,

"This is not an old banger," and promptly sat down. I had done my homework and my max was twenty six K. The bidding started at eight thousand and rose in bids of two thousand until it reached its market value of eighteen thousand. There was a moment's silence before I raised my hand and the bids started again and stopped at twenty eight thousand made by Ron Patterson an estate agent. I was visibility sweating, what to do? I hated breaking my own rules and was fully aware that a further bid would put me on a collision course with my bank manager.

For some reason I looked at Rebecca who simply smiled and seemed to nod her head as if to say "Go for it". I found myself raising my hand again.

"Thirty thousand," Bill said eagerly.

Thankfully there were no other bids. Suzy came over and handed me an envelope which contained the keys and papers, planting a big wet kiss on my lips to roars of approval from the male guests, I handed her a cheque for thirty big ones, writing the cheque was the painless part, facing my bank manager Jonathan Blight in a few days time, would be a different matter. Jonathan wasn't really a car man and drove an old grey Skoda. I would collect the Jag tomorrow, once I had sorted the paper work and had the car insured and taxed, I understood it had been fully serviced and had a twelve month MOT, ready to go! But would I be able to afford the petrol? I thought consuming my second glass of wine in one mighty gulp. When I regained my senses I looked up, Rebecca was sat smiling at me.

"What excitement," she said. "I thought for one moment you were going to faint, are you alright?"

"Yes," I replied, "I nearly did faint, I am not sure what came over me."

"Suzy's breasts in your face for one and more importantly big Boys with their toys, I would imagine," she said with a smile.

"Yes an expensive toy."

"A little like my ear rings."

"Yes, may I see them?"

"I'll show you mine if you show me yours."

"I would love to but mines locked up in a garage, I suspect in Kensington."

"Then we will have to wait until tomorrow," she said smiling. "I don't live far from Kensington, you could pick me up and we could have lunch, my treat, anyway I have a proposition for you, one I think you may be interested in."

"It's a while since I have been propositioned, I'm game," I said fascinated.

The auction came to an end around ten thirty and the guests began to leave at first in dribs and drabs and by eleven there was a queue leading out to the cloakroom. I was standing behind Rebecca when I felt a tap on my shoulder. I turned around to see Charles smiling face.

"David," he said shaking my hand.

"Be so kind as to pop by Monday morning, about eleven, there's something of interest I would like to discuss with you." He paused as if gauging my reaction to his polite command.

"Of course," I replied.

"Good man," he said adding, "I like your little Kandinsky. Barbara said it would look rather nice in our bedroom. See you Monday." We shook hands again and I turned back to Rebecca.

"Who's been a good boy then?" I noticed Rebecca's eyes, they weren't dark brown as I suspected but they were amber, and they were smiling at me.

"Oh it won't last, probably wants a freebie."

"What time are you picking me up David?"

"To suit you, I should have picked the car up by twelve and could be with you between twelve thirty and one o'clock."

"That would be perfect. See you tomorrow then."

I watched her take her coat and make her way out. Looking at the business card she had handed me. Apart from the address and phone number it just read Rebecca Davis Consultant. I took a taxi back to my flat in Saint Johns Wood. It had been a strange evening, not altogether my cup of tea but I had bought a great car even if I could not afford it, I was in Charles Patterson's good books and had met the intriguing Rebecca Davis. I wondered where we would go for lunch. It had become cold when I got out of the taxi at five to twelve; I hurried across the road, found the key to the flat, once inside I made my way to the drinks cabinet in the lounge and poured myself a large whiskey which I took with me to my bedroom. I spent the next twenty minutes thinking of the restaurants I had been to, nothing seemed good enough, I didn't want to rely on Rebecca to find a place to eat, but of course by not socialising I was out of touch. Tired, I fell asleep the whiskey half drunk, left on the bedside table beside the phone.

Chapter 2

22nd December 2015

I woke up next morning, clear headed and full of the joys of spring, quickly showered dressed, consumed two slices of toast, two cups of coffee and I was away flagging down a taxi to take me to Kensington. The XJ6 was parked on the forecourt and as I walked up to it, it looked magnificent. It was dove grey, not a mark or scratch in sight, with a cream leather interior and walnut dash. Winston Reid came over wearing bright blue overalls and a big grin on his face.

"You've got a beauty there my old son, forty thou on the clock one lady owner."

I looked at the log book; it had been purchased by Rupert Green who owned Greens Landscaping for his wife Julia on her fortieth birthday. Rupert was the main landscape contractor for Berkshire Developments in the south of England and was a very wealthy man, like me he was unprepared for the changes which were to befall him when in August this year and three years after her forty first birthday Julia died of Breast Cancer, we all attended the funeral. Rupert could not bring himself to either drive the Jag or sell it, in the end he decided to put it in the 'Save the Children auction. It was a magnificent gesture on his part and in due course I would write to him and express my pleasure at having purchased the car. I smiled and said,

"Thanks Winston," as we shook hands.

We finalised the details of the log book and with a flourish that took me by surprise I drove her of the forecourt and as smooth as silk glided into the busy traffic, I headed towards Rebecca's flat in Kensington Church Street. She was stood waiting by the ornate iron and cream coloured pumps. Style perfection, I thought.

"Umm, I like," she said as she got in. "Worth every penny."

"Where to Rebecca?"

"Straight on David, I'll tell you when to turn off. We are heading for Esher."

Little was said on the journey to Esher. I pulled into Esher Park Avenue and parked up in front of a derelict bungalow with substantial detached houses either side.

"This is it," Rebecca said. "I am looking to demolish the bungalow and build my dream home here, and I would like you to design it for me, but we have to get our skates on, I have an option to buy the land which runs out at the end of January. I know it's a bit of an imposition but I really would like you to design it for me."

"Not Richard Brown's company or Arkwright Associates," I teased.

"No, Richards a fantastic builder David and he will be my builder, but he's not an Architect and Reg Arkwright though good by most peoples standards, does not listen and you end up with having to live with what he thinks you will like. No, I want someone that listens and has flair to undertake the design."

She looked at me with a sweet smile, how could I refuse.

"Anyway," she added, handing me an envelope, "I thought this might come in handy."

I opened the envelope and there was a cheque made out to me for the sum of four thousand pounds. I had to smile.

"How did you work out I needed this sum exactly, before the bank manager chopped my head off?"

"That was easy David, when the bidding stopped at twenty six thou your bid I believe I watched you agonising over the following bid of twenty eight thou. It was simple reasoning that the money required to make up the thirty thousand smackers was not there, like Mr Micawber in Charles Dickens novel, David Copperfield, you hoped something would turn up David, and in your case it turned out to be me."

I was laughing and looking at her at the same time, her face was a picture of pure intrigue, her eyes told me she was playing with me, I wanted to kiss her there and then but for some reason I held back, should one kiss their new client, however beautiful?

"You don't need to give me all this Rebecca, I can manage," I said blushing.

"Yes perhaps you can, but what I am asking means you will have to work over the holidays and in the grand scheme of things it's not such a large percentage of the build costs. Anyway the four thousand is for the scheme drawings only.

"I'll need a brief Rebecca."

"Yes, I know we can discuss that over lunch and it's my turn to drive once we have walked the plot."

We started walking around the site, it was a good size I guessed seventy five to eighty metres wide and about two hundred and thirty metres front to back, the land was basically level, grassed over with a few small saplings. At the rear the garden was walled to a height of approximately two metres, a feature on its own. A house which I suspected the local town planners would like to be in keeping with the street scene would sit nicely on the plot without giving the feeling of being cramped. I took a few photos with my mobile phone and said I would get an AutoCAD ordinance copy of the site as soon as we went back to the car, then I would be able to start straight away without having to do a measured survey, the detailed survey would come later. As we walked back to the car I asked, "Why Esher Rebecca?"

She paused for a moment; she had the most beguiling smile.

"Well Esher's rather nice David, smart shops, it's refined, quiet and I like the nineteen twenties to nineteen thirties style of domestic architecture, to my mind, its suburbia honed to perfection. It's close to London, where I work, great train service, most of the time, and Esher's in the country, it's close to Portsmouth and the south coast, I have friends in Brighton, Hove and Eastbourne and I love going to visit the historic town of Portsmouth."

She looked back at the site, "It was always going to be either Esher or Cobham, I think Esher is classier and has all the facilities I need. Cobham is becoming full of footballers and their wags, not really my cup of tea."

We stood at the car.

"Do you think I am a snob David?"

"No I wouldn't say you're a snob, I would say you are very clever and astute."

"Thank you, I take that as a compliment," she said, touching my arm.

"PPP have many international clients and partners abroad and when it comes to hosting clients and partners visiting us, Japanese in particular, PPP prefer the personal touch, apparently the Japanese don't like hotels either, I can earn ten thousand pounds per week for allowing a Japanese delegation of five delegates to stay at the new house, that's once it's completed. Also the Japanese are mad keen on their horse racing and with me bed hopping into the bedroom in the flat over the garage, I will be on hand to escort them to either Sandown Park or Epsom Downs race courses. I get to see the racing from the members enclosure free and pocket six K per week is a tidy sum don't you think?"

"You've got it all worked out Rebecca," I said, admiring her business acumen.

"No, not always all but I try. That's why I want you to design the house for me, I've seen other house designs of yours, and the real thing, the houses you designed for BD, Richard Brown built in Richmond and Dorking, I have to hand it to you, there're smart but in an understated way, I like that."

It was my turn to say thank you, she was still smiling her beguiling smile.

"What else do you know about me Rebecca?"

I was smiling in my own playful way.

"Oh everything I need to know. I rarely take chances in relationships either business or personal and as far as Architects are concerned you come highly recommended and as for the personal side of things, well I admit I have gone out on a limb with you so we will just have to wait and see.

"Touché," I replied. We got to the car.

"It's my turn to drive," she said and I tossed her the keys, whilst she drove to the rendezvous for our lunch I made a couple of calls, one to the ordinance map suppliers and then to my bank manager.

"Do you have enough money to buy lunch or is it going to be baked beans on toast?"

"I think I have enough for double egg and chips or 'Captain Birds Eye' fish fingers and mushy peas at a greasy spoon in North Acton, they also do an all day breakfast, all you can eat for a fiver includes two slices of black pudding." I tried to look serious as I spoke. Rebecca was laughing and I knew we were going to have a wonderful day. We didn't have far to drive, She headed back towards London and we stopped at a rather nice looking Restaurant at Hampton Hill called 'La Famillia' a Spanish restaurant that Rebecca said she had tried once before and hoped I would like.

She parked up expertly into a tiny space that I would not have dared to try. It was amazing how quickly time flies it was just three o'clock the time the restaurant opened. We were shown to a table for two and ordered drinks, I had tonic water and Rebecca had a lime and soda. We both decided on the chicken for a main course.

Whist we were waiting, I asked Rebecca to give me outlines for the brief for the house. She understood that the house needed to be in keeping with its neighbours and would be less likely to hit the buffers when it came to getting full Planning permission, it already had outline approval for a five bed-roomed dwelling. She handed me a piece of typed paper, which was the basis of the brief. Entrance hall, two reception rooms at front, large kitchen and dining room, utility room, ground floor toilet and shower room, coats cupboard, pantry, stairs leading to first floor, integral access to garages one side and workshop storage other side, small basement incorporating boiler room and wine cellar. First floor, five bedrooms en-suite the master bedroom was to have walk-in dressing rooms and small sitting areas. The roof space over the garage and store rooms were to access from ground floor for live in cook house keeper and gardener/janitor. The garden at the front was to have a carriage drive, the gardens at the rear were to have a kitchen vegetable garden and substantial greenhouse and at the bottom of the garden a small summer house with mini kitchen and toilet facilities. The lawn at the rear should be suitable to play croquet.

"I'm surprised you haven't drawn up the plans yourself," I said as our main course arrived.

"Yes I know what I want but like Richard I'm not an architect and when I heard about how you enjoy listening and engaging in your clients ideas rather than heaping on your own 'what's good for you blurb' I knew you were the right person."

"Is everything that simple Rebecca?"

"Business wise yes, and that's the key, keep things simple."

The food was wonderful and the restaurant had a nice atmosphere. We gave the conversation a rest whilst we enjoyed the food. For dessert, Rebecca had strawberries and ice cream whilst I had lemon tart and cream. We ordered a cafetiere and relaxed just enjoying the atmosphere and each others company. We had our first little argument over who was paying for lunch and eventually she allowed me to pay on the condition that when I had some drawings to show her she would entertain me with lunch at her flat. I couldn't wait to see her flat, and I think she knew it, I was enthralled and it showed, I felt good, the first time in a long while and unless Rebecca took offence I was happy for her to see my pleasure of her company. We headed back to London, most of the traffic was heading in the opposite direction and I found myself pulling up outside a rather smart block of flats.

"That's me, the one on the end third floor up." She pointed. The one with the blinds. We stood for a few moments saying nothing, I guess she was waiting to see how I was going to say good bye for now, I moved gently towards her took her hand

and kissed her on the cheek.

"Is that the best you can do David? I was expecting a real smacker."

"I guess I'm out of practice," I replied and we kissed again, gently but meaningfully.

"Umm that's better."

"Thank you," I said, "for a wonderful day, I'll be in touch as soon as…"

She cut me short. "Don't leave it too long then," she said smiling as she opened the gate and walked up the footpath to the entrance doors.

"Bye," I said but she didn't hear me, and then she was gone.

Chapter 3

Christmas December 2015

I had never been much of a one for Christmas and less so after Jane's death. I was pleased I had something to do and get me through the empty days. My parents were both dead, I had no brothers or sisters and Jane's parents, still alive blamed me for their daughter's death which was ridiculous, I knew Jane was ill, I could tell by how tired she became, hew skin had lost its shine and colour; she was deathly thin and wouldn't eat. I had begged her to get an appointment to see the Doctor, but she refused to listen, Her mother, Freda was a bombastic woman and also a bully, she liked to talk but like Jane would not listen had never really taken to me, saying I should have insisted she see a doctor and it was my fault the cancer had spread to a point where it became terminal. From the very beginning when we were courting, Jane's mother made it very clear she did not approve of me. After the wedding ceremony I had as a token of respect called her mum. Luckily no one else was around when she said,

"David, I am not your mother and don't ever refer to me as mum. As and when we have to see you, please call me Freda and call Jane's father Benjamin, not Ben or Benny, do you understand?"

She gave me the most awful of looks. Like I was a piece of dirt on her shoe, I was gob smacked and spluttered out,

"Yes of course Freda."

At that moment Jane and her father appeared, Freda was all smiles; Jane took my hand and said,

"I am so happy mum."

"Yes well," Freda said composing herself and forcing a smile. "I'll go and see about the cake."

I could see the look of anger on Jane's face. Has mum said anything to upset you David?"

"No everything's just fine Jane, I think its been a long day for her." Jane's father Benjamin who had retired early from teaching due to stress was of no help allowing his wife to make the wild accusations but she wouldn't listen to him when he had the bottle to say she was being unfair, she would give him a withering look which made him appear to visibly shrink, and whatever I said in my defence would never have been enough. So we don't exchange Christmas cards any more. I believe they moved from Barnet to somewhere in Shropshire, I never saw or heard from them again after Jane's funeral. I have a cousin that lives in Durham and that's about as far as my family goes, in some ways it suits me. I am a bit of a loner and don't like having to explain myself or give a running commentary on how well I am coping. Now for the first time in six years I had someone and something to occupy my mind, Rebecca and her plans for a house in Esher. I finished my drawings for Richard Brown on the twenty third of December and threw myself into the design of Rebecca's house. I down loaded the photos of the site and street scene and copied them onto the auto cad drawing, scaled them down to fit the scale of the drawing I could do later. I wanted to show how the house would fit in with the adjacent properties. I had found in the past that neighbours could be difficult if ignored and I wanted the new house to blend in, subject of course to Rebecca's approval. I listened to my favourite music, John Prine's, 'Harvest' album, Kate and Ann Mcgarrigle's 'Dancer with bruised knees' and Emmylou Harris's Bluebird' album, all singer song writers singing, simple heart felt folk and country songs about life, love and betrayal, spending the next three days engrossed in the plans of the house. I didn't go out or speak to anybody on the phone, I was lost in a world of my own, at peace with myself, something I had not enjoyed in a long time. The house was designed on traditional lines with internal and external load bearing cavity walls supporting the floors and walls on concrete strip foundations. The ground floor comprised timber panelled flooring on tongued and grooved floor boards on timber joists with an insulated air gap and over site concrete, I am a great believer in traditional construction which allowed a house to breath, something which I considered essential in our ever changing climate, this was helped by traditional fire places in the dining and reception rooms. The double glazed windows were of hardwood painted white. I had chosen a soft red brick for the ground floor and a cream render at first floor, a sandy coloured brick for the garage and workshop buildings either side of the house. The pitched roof was tiled with rosemary tiles with white fascia, soffit boards and traditional cast iron guttering and rainwater pipes, I was aiming for a clean, smart warm looking house. The house was set back from the road and the shingle carriage drive added to the warm look, between the out buildings and the house there were Californian screen blocks which allowed a certain amount of light and a view into the courtyards whilst maintaining their privacy. Of course Rebecca would need to approve the designs and materials but we had discussed her ideas on what she likes and I was confident the proposals would meet with her approval; we would have to wait and see. When I was satisfied with the house design, on Boxing Day I turned my attention to making a small model of the proposals and then taking photos from different angles to show the house to its best effect. All the while in the back of my mind was Rebecca, how easy she was to be with and how it seemed to me she wanted me as much as I wanted her. The money she had given me for the work played on my mind in different ways, I would have gladly have done the work for nothing but I did need the money, was that so bad of me? Sometimes I thought yes and then I found myself thinking no and then I found myself thinking of our kiss and how her body moulded into mine as she leaned forward, was I being unfaithful to Jane's memory? Should I go for it? Was Rebecca just playing a game? Two bottles of scotch in three days told me that I was puddled and had no clear sense of direction, what did stand out was the house design, if I may say so, it looked every bit as good as I hoped it would when I first saw the site. I was seeing Charles Patterson tomorrow and wanted to be ship shape so I eased down on the booze, I also wanted to speak to Rebecca but I had the impression she did not want to speak to me before the twenty ninth, odd that really. Charlie Patterson was a self made man who from a secondary school education studied at night whilst working for a company of building surveyors to get his Higher National Diploma and then pass his exams to become a chartered surveyor. By comparison my journey to become a chartered architect was a breeze. My parents were relatively well off and I attended St Judes private school before obtaining my O and A levels and then straight to University to Study architecture. My father was a builder and it was through him I took up my first post as an Architect for Wallis Jones and Stackman in Stanmore. My father did most of their refurbishment work and two projects one for Betty and Charlie Patterson at their home in Bishops Gate and then, their offices in Marble Arch put me on the map. Mr Patterson as I called Charlie in those days was a good client and suggested I was wasting my time at Wallis Jones and Stackman. We had always got on well and it was Charlie who suggested to Richard Brown one of his favoured Building Contractors that he should employ me as his Architect so I set up shop in the offices over my fathers builders yard in Edgware. When my parents died I inherited their house and the builders yard which I initially leased out, but keeping the garage, and purchased a flat in St Johns Wood and a small suite of offices close by, I enjoyed my new status as an architect with my own practice, I employed a trainee architect, Jason Hill a clean cut young man eager to listen and learn and Mary Wiltshire a single mum with a boy Adam aged six, Mary was willing and loyal and we fitted around her requirements where Adam was concerned. Flexibility worked both ways in my book, she worked five mornings a week to man the telephones and keep abreast of the filing, her memory was better than Jason and mine put together. We were a small and efficient team, we went on from there. There were plenty of freelance architects and technicians if the work load became too heavy, though in the main with Jason's and Mary's help we managed fine. Charlie had moved to Berkshire Developments when it was a one man band owned by Peter Clarke, who saw in Charlie the mirror image of himself. Under Peter's stewardship Berkshire Developments grew at a phenomenal rate. Charlie was also a natural business man as well as being a brilliant surveyor. Together they became one of the largest developers in the country. They started out with offices over a green grocers in Shepherds Bush before moving on to a suite of offices near Marble Arch and finally to Brooke Street, Mayfair. When Peter retired due to ill health, Charlie became chairman. He was a genial sort of man and was liked and respected by his staff and people in the industry. Five ten slightly over weight he cast an imposing figure! Always well dressed he didn't tolerate sloppiness or lateness of those he employed. His wife Betty two years younger than him was successful in her own right, with a typing agency and had been awarded an MBE for her work running the Berkshire Development Foundation for 'Save the Children'. As the foundation took more and more of her time she handed over the reigns of the agency to her Sister Brenda. I set off to meet Charles at his Brook Street offices at nine thirty and arrived in good time. Ten forty five and waited patiently in the reception until he was ready to see me. What I liked about Charles Patterson was that he had never lost sight of his roots, where he came from and the people he had grown up with as a boy. He didn't have airs and graces, he treated people fairly and though enjoying the life bought with a successful business he shared much of his wealth. Staff were well paid and shared in a bonus scheme and surplus wealth was directed to his favourite charity 'Save the Children.' He had been brought up in Stonebridge Park and knew what it was like to live in a rough area, unlike many he survived and was a better man for it. At eleven precisely, Dawn his PA ushered me into his offices.

"David thanks for coming," he said in his booming voice, "have a seat."

"Dawn two coffees please and no calls."

He looked at me like he was assessing a dog at crufts, was I a pedigree?

Charles didn't waste time with idle chit chat but got straight to the point.

"You might have heard the rumours David, but change is on the way at Berkshire Developments, we need to be more ship shape, too many stragglers not pulling there weight, too much in fighting between Designers and Contractors. In a nut shell by this time next year I believe fifty percent of the existing designers and contractors we currently employ will be looking elsewhere for their bread and butter, unless with your assistance they are capable of change."

Dawn came in with a silver tray of coffee and some walnut whirls and shortbread, both my favourites.

"Cream or Milk David?"

She stood to the side of me making sure I could admire her ample bust from the gap in her blouse, Charles watched amused, he had obviously seen the show many times before. I made sure I did not move until she had poured the coffee and closed the door behind her.

"What it comes down to David is that we need a man who can wield the axe, so to speak which is where you come in."

"I'm not sure I follow Charles I am an Architect not a lumberjack."

"Point taken, yes I know that, but I mean, and by I, I mean we the Board of Directors wants you to join Berkshire Developments as a Senior Project Manager who will ferret out the stragglers and good for nothings so we can move on, faster, better organised, ready for when we become a Plc."

I went to say something but he waved his hand and said, "Hear me out David before you say anything else." He chomped on a walnut whip. A minute later, after furious chewing he carried on.

"We want you to join Berkshire in an important roll noted by the salary we are offering you, one hundred and seventy thousand pounds per year, and a six year contract with an initial signing on fee of twenty five K. You will also have a class A car provided, you can keep the Jag for weekends, Bupa insurance and a bonus of fifty thousand pound per year based on performance. I estimate that at present you gross about seventy to eighty K." He sat smugly swallowing a third walnut whirl. All my problems it seemed were resolved in one fifteen minute interview, except for Rebecca, the job would entail a considerable amount of time on the road, when would I get the time to see her?

"Can I have twenty four hours Charles to think about it?"

"Yes David but not a minute longer though, I have men by the cart load and two women one from Turkey and one from Scotland, from the Cameroun clan throwing themselves off bridges and trains to get this job."

"Understood Charles, I will phone you tomorrow, before eleven."

We said our good-bye's and shook hands; Dawn was waiting at the door by the mistletoe. I gave her a quick peck but Dawn had other ideas, she wanted the full works and said so, being a gentleman I felt obliged to respond. Her lips and tongue began to work away furiously.

"Yum," she said wanting another kiss but I managed to prize her arms from me and made some remark about my blood pressure, she reluctantly let me go. Another person to keep on side, I wouldn't want Dawn as an enemy.

As soon as I got home I rang Rebecca. "Good morning," she said lazily.

I sensed she was still in bed or had just got up, its afternoon Rebecca its 1 o'clock."

"Oh, good afternoon then."

I have some drawings and a model of the house to show you and I have something I would like to get your opinion on."

"Today?"

"Yes today would be best if you could make it, I have just seen Charles Patterson and he has made me a proposition and I would like to discuss it with you before I get back to him tomorrow.

"Did you want to come here or me come to you?"

"I don't mind but it might be easier if I come to you."

"Okay, come over about three, give me time to have a shower

and tidy up."

"Thanks, Rebecca, see you about three."

I went into my small study, I used as an office when at home and took the plans I had printed off and also covered the model in cling film and took them to the car.

Should I buy a bottle of wine or something? I decided no, might be seen as a little pushy. I changed into some grey slacks a white shirt and took my blue blazer from the wardrobe. I decided against a tie, we were officially still on holiday so I wore my blue loafers. It took me a little longer than I thought to get from St Johns wood to Kensington and I pulled up outside the block of flats where Rebecca lived at five to three. I rang her on my mobile and asked if she could come down, I couldn't carry the model and the drawings together, she sounded excited and two minutes later she came over to the car wearing a pair of strawberry red cropped pants, a white blouse and red pumps, she looked ravishing with her radiant smile focused on me, she came over and kissed me on the cheek saying.

"Hello, this looks interesting," she said looking at the model.

Taking the folder with the drawings and photos whilst I managed the model.

We made our way to the lifts and her flat; I was puffing by the time we got to her flat.

"You're not fit David, we'll have to get you to take some exercise."

There was a playful hint of what exercise might be, she was laughing and playing with me as we entered the living room.

"Put it down on the dining table David."

I carefully removed the cling film and sat the model on the table; it was to a scale of one to fifty and with the site boundaries, the board it sat on measured nine hundred mm by twelve hundred mm it was not so much heavy as cumbersome.

"Tea coffee? It's a bit early for wine, even for me," I smiled. "Coffee would be great."

My eyes scanned the room with its elegant Edwardian furniture and two small Pre- Raphaelite paintings, I went over to the window and looked down onto the empty street below; I could live here, it was smart and quiet, and it was where Rebecca lived, one step at a time old chap, I said to myself. Rebecca came in with a tray of coffee and shortbread which she put next to the model.

"Shall we look at the drawings first David?"

"Yes good idea."

We started with the ground floor "I said nothing giving her time to form some initial reaction.

"And the first floor David." I place another drawing in front of her.

She said nothing for several minutes and then asked for the elevations. Which I had drawn in colour.

"These are really fabulous David. I'm so pleased I was able to persuade you to prepare the drawings for me and at such short notice, we can discuss them in more detail in a minute."

She got up and stood over me.

"First you deserve a kiss." She leaned down and her lips softly brushed mine, that was it, but I was not going to complain. She sat back down and began turning the model around slowly.

"Can I keep this David, for a day or two?"

"Of course, you have paid for it."

"I didn't expect it would include a model, let me give you some more money."

"No Rebecca and that's final, I would be offended."

"Stay for supper then, I have a casserole in the oven."

"That I will agree to, but can I buy some wine?"

"Let me check." She went over to the sideboard. "I have half a bottle of Chardonnay, about a cup full of manky red a week old, yuck! Yes I think we will have to go to the corner shop, it's about a ten minute walk, are you fit enough? and if you have more than 1 glass I suppose you will want to stay over, I have a spare bedroom but you'll have to promise to behave yourself."

I had the impression she was playing with me again.

"I can manage on one glass, and I don't want to make any promises, I can't keep, you have this certain way of looking at me that makes me impulsive and."

"We don't want to go there, do we?" she smiled.

"Poor boy, can't behave himself, let's look at the drawings again and then we will get the wine."

I watched her as she looked at the drawings, "Do you know what I love most?"

"Yes, I think I can guess."

"The courtyards, it's so clever the way you have created them between the out buildings and the house. I am sure it will be wonderful to sit in a secluded space, well done David, I like the house design, as a treat I am going to take you out to dinner again soon, would you be willing to come to the council planners with me?"

"Of course, it would be a pleasure. You might take the model or photos of the model."

"What a good idea, let's go and get that wine, I need a drink."

We walked at a brisk pace to the local Spar shop, she slipped her arm through mine like we were a couple, and it felt natural. We bought one bottle of red and one bottle of white, it looked like I would not be going home, anyway I paid for the wine and we headed back to her flat. I must say I needed a drink as much as Rebecca when we final got to sit down, she was right, I wasn't fit.

"Red or white?" she asked a wicked smile on her face.

"Same as you, red please."

"I'm having white." I blushed. "That's what you get when you try to be too clever."

I said, "White then please."

She poured the wine into two large glasses so that by the time she had finished there was just over half a bottle left.

"I'm going to need my Jim jams if I have another one of those," I said adding, "cheers and a happy New Year Rebecca."

"Yes and cheers to you, and thank you so much for the wonderful house design, I'm going to get Richard to give me an estimate and then see the planners in the New Year."

She took a sip of her wine. "You mentioned over the phone there was something you wanted to run by me David?"

"Yes, Charles Patterson has offered me a job, wants me to join Berkshire Developments as a senior project manager overseeing the performance of all the contractors and designers, to ensure that they work together rather than all the present in fighting. It's a big salary one hundred and seventy K, six year contract and twenty five thousand pounds tax free, signing on fee. I have to give him an answer by eleven tomorrow morning."

"It sounds fantastic, why haven't you bitten his hand off, Jag paid for minus one K, is there a catch?"

"No, it's all kosher, however the job will involve quite a lot of travelling, I'm inclined to say yes of course but I was just beginning to think I might have a social life, sounds a bit silly I know but I have had six years in the wilderness, working yes but with no direction, I believe I am through that period of my life now and I don't want to spend the rest of my life driving up and down the M1 and coming home to an empty flat."

Rebecca did not say anything for a few moments; I could tell she was thinking, probably thinking I'm a nut case.

"I am not sure if you know what work I do David, I'm an auditor and have to spend time travelling up and down the M1 to visit Contractors and Designers also employed by Berkshire Developments mainly, so I know how demanding the job and travelling can be. I make sure I only travel Tuesdays, Wednesdays and Thursdays, this leaves me Monday and Friday, to complete my reports and sometimes Saturday mornings. Like you I am well paid for my services and my life has to a greater extent revolved around business, this suited me but I realise at sometime I will want more to life than producing reports. The house in Esher is a nest egg, I figure it will cost me around £950K all in and in six or seven years be worth around £2.8M to 3.8M when I sell up and retire."

"That's a good plan Rebecca."

"Is this someone you want to see more of, me? Or am I getting the wrong end of the stick?"

"Easy to spot I guess, yes I find you very attractive, interesting and we seem to get on well, what I am hoping is that you might feel the same as me and look forward to seeing our friendship develop, nothing more than that."

"I'm glad you put it like that, what I suggest when you see Charles tomorrow is that you tell him travelling needs to be limited to three days per week, so you can write up your reports as I do on the other two days, I think if he wants you badly enough, he will go for it, and in reply to your comment about us, if there is to be an us, then I suggest we take it slowly. I admit to having a certain how shall I say, a sense of excitement, expectation and pleasure, being with you, yes, we get on, that's for sure. However I am a cautious woman and don't want complications in my life. But If I am truthful I do like being kissed by you. Does that answer your question?"

Yes, it's what I hoped you would say, and thank you for being so forthright." My face was beaming with delight.

"I'm inclined to think Friday evenings, to Monday's should give us adequate time to develop our relationship, if there is to be one," she said.

I hadn't noticed but my glass was empty and so was Rebecca's. "Fill up?"

"Yes please." I handed her my glass.

"When are you planning to see Richard Brown about the budget costs for the house?"

"The second of January."

"Then, can I suggest we spend some time drawing up a

schedule of materials and finishes which can be added to the drawings or as a stand alone document. I find that this way you both have a clearer idea of what you are getting for your money."

"Good idea." I could tell she was impressed and so she should be.

"I have a standard template we can use if you give me some ideas of finishes you would like, fixtures and fittings tonight, I can work on that tomorrow morning and have a draft with you for the afternoon which would still give you time to look through it briefly on New Years day and unless there are not too many alterations, I can have the document back to you mid morning on the second."

"That's a good idea, David, let me get a pen and note pad, where do we start?"

"Room by room, floor finishes, walls, ceilings, fixtures and fittings, items like doors and windows I would expect to come under one heading i.e. say American oak for staircase, door, and frames, satin finish fitted with locks and lever furniture and hardwood windows painted white complete with double glazing, opening lights, and security locks to opening windows, etc.

"I realise what you mean, we need to identify the standards otherwise we might end up with just ordinary finishes, not that Richard skimps."

"I agree but this does no harm and focuses your mind on the detail you want and expect and what you are prepared to pay for. We moved back to the dining room table and began looking at the plan of the ground floor.

"Oh I almost forgot David, what time would you like to eat?"

"To suit you, shall we make a start and see how we go then stop for dinner?

Rebecca was an excellent client and had a clear vision of what she wanted and how the house should look when finished. The value of having a schedule was born out when it came to whether she wanted cornices between walls and ceiling, picture rails, blinds and or curtain rails to windows, which in her case was yes to all. These small items can add up in terms of cost and the more you can identify now the more accurate the budget cost will be. There is also the time element for the build; the greater detail the longer the build will take.

"I like all of it, my only concern is your having to work tomorrow."

"Not a problem, let's get as close as we can before you commit to buying."

"I really appreciate what you are doing for me, David."

"Good, more wine please."

"It was eight o'clock when we finished and we were down to one third of the second bottle of red and hadn't eaten, I was famished and ready for the chicken casserole which was superb, I mopped up the gravy with chunks of bread to Rebecca's delight.

By ten thirty we had consumed both bottles of wine and a third of a bottle of dry sherry and we were both exhausted. We kissed quite passionately then I made my way to the guest room, it was a strange feeling. We had kissed and wished each other good night and gone to separate rooms. I lay on the bed and stared up at the ceiling, wondering what she was thinking, my head was buzzing and knew it would be a while before I slept. I wasn't drunk but mellow. I played the days events over in my mind, She had made it abundantly clear she would not be rushed; I think if I was honest going to bed with Rebecca would be fantastic but getting a relationship right, one that would last was a different kettle of fish. It frightened me a little that I was thinking long term when I had only known her a few days but everything seemed perfect, I thought of Rebecca in her bed the other side of the partition, in truth I would like to have been laying beside her, I could still smell her perfume, what a wonderful day, eventually I fell asleep.

Chapter 4
30th December 2015

I woke to the sound of Rebecca passing my room. I got up and made enough noise for her to know I was up and about.

I washed and dressed quickly and noticed a tooth brush on my bedside table which I used, borrowing her tooth paste.

As I entered the kitchen, I was greeted by the smell of fresh coffee and a quick kiss from Rebecca. I could get used to this but it wasn't the time to express my thoughts. We had toast and coffee and then we set off for my place so we could get the fixtures, fittings and finishes schedule updated on the computer and printed off ready for Rebecca's meeting with Richard Brown. Whilst Rebecca drove, I phoned Charlie and said I would be pleased to take the job.

"Good man," he said. "Come in on the fifth and we will get you set up. I'll speak to Richard Brown and explain the situation, be interesting to see who is his new Architect might be. Not too much happens in January, so you will have time to tidy up and hand over any outstanding issues."

"Thanks Charles," I said.

"See you on the fifth David."

I didn't need to give Rebecca direction's she knew the road I lived on. "Number thirty is it David?"

"That's the one," I said, she parked up and we made our way to my first floor flat.

I couldn't remember how I had left it and was relieved to find it was reasonably tidy.

"This is nice David," she said walking from the hall, through the living room to the kitchen.

"It suits me," I replied.

We had some more coffee and then set about working up the schedule of fixtures, fittings and finishes for her new house. Once Rebecca saw how easy it was to develop the schedule she took over the typing. By lunch time we had the document pretty much finished and ready for printing.

We broke off for lunch and I let loose my cooking skills which comprised omelette and chips, not very original but we were both hungry. After lunch we set about printing off five copies of the drawings and schedule which we wire bound, two copies for her, two for Richard and one for me.

I then put everything on to two CDR'S, one for Rebecca and one for Richard's use.

By four o'clock, we had had enough and set back off for Kensington, to take Rebecca back to her flat. Tomorrow was New Year's Eve and she asked me if I would like to come over for dinner. We agreed I would come over for eight and we would dine about nine. We kissed and said good bye. I felt odd as I walked back to the car.

We had been together for best part of twenty four hours and now I was back to being alone and I didn't have the guts to say "Hey Rebecca let's go somewhere today."

If truth be known I feared rejection, what a wimp but I also knew Rebecca would not be cajoled, if I wanted more than a kiss, or a night in bed, then I would have to be patient. I suspected that some time ago she had been hurt or let down by a man, what was so special about me? Absolutely nothing, in the grand scheme of things I was like everyone else, ordinary, that wasn't a put down, it was how I saw myself and most people I had met. I believe most of us do the same things mainly, if anything marks us out, it is selflessness, commitment, giving without the need for reward, in my book, that's special. I have little time for people that say look at me or keep their hands in their pockets when it's their round, I've always hated meanness.

That's one of the things I liked about Rebecca, she wanted to help me when she surmised I had a cash flow problem of my own making I may add, and gave me some money. I liked that, I would have helped her with her plans for her house for nothing as a friend of a friend, the friend being Charlie Patterson. When we were together I felt alive something I hadn't properly felt since Jane's death. Now I was bursting with excitement but I figured it would be a while before Rebecca let her guard down and she felt the same way as me. I was tired when I got home though it was only three o'clock. I rarely check my emails other than when I am at work but for some reason I opened the in box. There was an email, it was from Rebecca. I thought the worst for a moment, thinking it was a 'dear John' letter but pleased to find when reading her letter, I was way off beam.

Dear David

I just wanted to let you know how much I appreciate all you have done for me over the past few days.

The design of the house is flawless and I am very excited, thank you I also wanted to say how much I have enjoyed your company. It has been a very long time since I spent as much time with a man as we have spent over the last few days and I was deeply moved that you wanted to speak to me about how we might fair when you have been offered a new career.

Like still waters your expression of caring runs deep in me.

If you can give me a little time for things to sink in, I am sure we will be fine and our friendship and dare I say 'love' will flourish. I am looking forward to tomorrow and the beginning of a new year.

Rebecca x

PS please wear your DJ for dinner tomorrow, I love black tie affairs.

I was gob smacked and elated at the same time. Of course I wanted to reply to her email straight away.

Dear Rebecca

Thank you so much for your heart warming email, what a wonderful surprise. I take on board fully your request for time, I have been nowhere other than work for a long while and being patient for something as you say we both want, is the best way forward. There is no rush and we can move forward at a pace that suits you.

I had intended to wear my DJ and dickey bow so you have saved me a call. Looking forward to dinner and seeing the New Year in with you.

With much affection

David x

I read and re-read my e mail several times, changing the odd word before pressing the send button. Now tomorrow evening did not seem so far away.

It was ten thirty when I called it a day and went to bed anticipating another restless night but I fell asleep within minutes.

Chapter 5
New Years Eve 2015

I spent most of New Years eve in an up-beat mood, thinking about how I would approach assessing a Berkshire Developments Contractor's and Designer's and began to develop a template of questions which would assist in making my reports and recommendations as to their viability as part of the Berkshire Developments list of approved contractors and designers. I felt it was important that each company was asked to address the same issues and questions to ensure an assessment was not arbitrary. The issue with most building projects was the blame game when something went wrong. This was the main reason companies like Berkshire Developments preferred 'Design and Build' as the way to award a contract. That way they were dealing with one organisation if something went wrong with the services or the windows failed and misted up, BD didn't care if it was the main Contractor or his sub-contractor that was at fault, it was the main contractor who had to put it right. In some cases the Architect who had prepared the scheme drawings and obtained planning permission would be novated as the Architect for the works and would be employed by the main contractor as would all the other specialist designers. The main contractor was also responsible for delivering the build on time, another big plus for Clients. Main Contractors liked this type of contract; it gives them control of the project. Sometimes to achieve program or budgetary requirements they would bully their sub-contractors and designers into cutting corners and then coming for them at a later date when something went wrong, usually falling behind unrealistic program. Sequence of work, drying out times, testing and commissioning of services were often the main issues. The Main Contractor not wanting to take the blame for their haste, when with a little more time at the design stage, the mistakes would have been avoided became the bad guy, brow beating his designers and sub contractors into submission. I was being employed to make sure these issues didn't arise and to weed out the trouble makers whoever they were. I wasn't going to be a popular person and I would need my diplomatic skills to ensure I did not make things worse. It was going to be a challenge, working for Richard Brown had been good, he gave me time and space to deliver the detailed design, he listened when he thought my advice might be of value, we liked each other and got on. This was not the case with all of those employed by Berkshire Developments, it was well known that some main contractors deliberately employed bully boy site agents and aggressive surveyors who made the sub-contractors wish they hadn't been born. I spent a lot of time thinking about my initial approach, the art of the interview was to whet the contractors and designers appetite, talking about things in general not letting on concerns that may have filtered through the system and before someone cottoned on as to the depth and purpose of my investigation I had a picture of how their organisation worked, its concerns, and the type of people it employed. There had been many reports of site meetings where site representatives for sub-contractors had squared up to the main contractors project manager, his surveyor or site agent when things go nasty and payments were deliberately delayed or pending litigation with held whilst the main contractor wanted more and more performance for less and less money, usually when the project was running over budget and or behind program. It soon came round to six o'clock and I wrapped up shop and got ready to see Rebecca. I had a go at pressing my DJ and gave it up as a bad job. By seven however, I was spic and span, having managed to tie my new dickey bow and left my flat setting off for Rebecca's. As I came into Kensington High Street I took a left turn and stopped outside the Spar shop we had been to two days before to buy the wine. On the forecourt were buckets of flowers and I picked up the last bunch of long stem red roses and went inside. The only Champagne they had was thirty five pounds a bottle; I purchased that and the roses and made my way back to the car. I was lucky enough to find a space in front of the flats and pressed the intercom and Rebecca buzzed me up. She opened the front door as I was about to turn the lever handle on the door, she looked jaw dropping beautiful, wearing a calf length cream dress, square cut neck line, three quarter length sleeves and soft brown court shoes, her smile was radiant as she came forward and kissed me, taking the flowers as we made our way to the kitchen. I put the Champagne in the fridge and as I turned I noticed Rebecca was wiping a tear from her cheek.

"Are you okay?" I asked.

She smiled putting the roses down on the worktop.

"Yes I'm fine, it's just the roses, they are so beautiful David, you'll be wondering what you have got yourself into, this is the second time I have shed a tear today, the first time was when I received your email, I need to pull myself together."

"There is nothing wrong with expressing emotion; I think it's healthy actually." She smiled again.

"I wish sometimes you weren't so kind and understanding, it un- nerves me a little, I guess I am not used to it."

"Let's have a glass of wine and sit for a moment."

She rested her head on my shoulder as we made our way into the living room and sat beside each other on her sumptuous green chesterfield.

“It’s been quite a week, one way or another,” she said taking a sip of her wine.

“Yes it will take some getting used to, what are we having to eat?” I said, trying to lighten the atmosphere.

“Duck breasts with orange sauce, red cabbage with nutmeg, red berries, peas and parmentier potatoes.”

“Sounds good, can I help?”

“No, I’ll be fine.” She took another sip of wine. “Do you believe in fate?” Rebecca asked.

“Yes, in part I do.”

“How do you mean David?”

“Well in our case for instance, it might have been fate that lead us to meeting at Charlie’s do and being on the same table, but what happens next, once we have met, I believe is down to us.”

“Yes, I think pretty much along the same lines. You’re very sweet David.” She gave me a quick kiss, got up and made her way to the kitchen.

“You can put the bubbly in the cooler if you want to be helpful.”

I was pretty sure the moment of reflection was over as I picked up the Champagne and placed it in the cooler. “You can also trim the roses and put them in a vase.” She was smiling and opening the oven to check the duck. I took the roses to the other side of the kitchen, found the vase in the sideboard and began removing the lower leaves and paring the bottom of the stems.

“How did you spend your day David?” She was telling me in her coded way she was fine.

“I have begun working up some ideas for the new job, working on a format for when I visit Contractors and Designers. Now I have agreed to work for BD I am looking forward to it. The only issues I have are what to do about Jason, he's my tech he has been with me for ten years and I need to let Charles know I have one outstanding commission, I want to complete."

"The house in Esher?"

"Yes that's the one, I realise that Richard will take over the design if you go ahead but I want to be able to go with you to the planners without feeling I am not focusing on my work at BD."

I agree about the house, Charles can be funny if he thinks you are working on the side, as for Jason I am sure Charles will understand you need someone in the office to run things whilst you are away."

"Yes, but he might have someone else in mind."

"Right, well the duck breasts are about done other than letting them rest, we can start serving up if you like and take the wine in please, I bought some Merlot, and I hope you like it?"

"Its one of my favourite red wines." In truth although I had had Merlot before, I could not tell one red from another. I took the wine from the small rack, uncorked it and took it into the dining room; the setting was beautiful and intimate.

"Shall I light the candles?" I asked.

"Yes please." She came in with the duck and two tureens containing the vegetables.

"Here we are."

I poured the wine as Rebecca served the duck breasts and vegetables.

"Cheers," I said. "To us."

"To us," she replied.

We ate in relative silence Miles Davis was playing quietly from the CD player, the candles flickered the light across the small dining table, I felt I could have been in heaven, everything was just perfect.

"This really is lovely," I said, "I love the duck."

"Its one of my favourites as well, but I think you need to be having a meal with someone to enjoy duck to the full, that's one of the few drawbacks of living alone and I do love cooking but not for myself to eat alone, I usually buy ready to cook meals if I am at home, it's nice to be cooking again."

In the candle light which flickered and danced across the table and on to us, Rebecca looked enchanting; it created a mood of intimacy, which I slightly diminished when I said.

"I know the feeling, it's double egg, cold ham and aunt Bessie's home made frozen chips for me." Rebecca laughed saying, "I can just picture you sitting alone at home with a plateful of chips and a mug of coffee. For desert Rebecca had made a New York cheese cake, which we had with single pouring cream it was delicious. We took our coffees into the living room, Charlie Parker had replaced Miles Davis on the gramophone and we sat quietly enjoying the music and our coffees, Rebecca had a brandy but I declined, it might be a long night and I didn't want to be nodding off.

It was just pleasant doing and saying nothing, as the minutes ran down to midnight. When the clock in the hall struck twelve we kissed and toasted each other with the Champagne, I think we both knew what would happen next but it was Rebecca's call, she has said she needed time and though I sensed this was the right time I wasn't going to force the pace. We kissed for what seemed a long time and when she looked up and smiled at me her eyes were a wash with tears.

"The third time in twenty four hours," she said, adding, "take me to bed David."

We kissed again and made our way to her bedroom. The light from the hall gave a soft glow to the bedroom. It had been a long time since I had been with a woman and I was unsure of my own emotions, I knew Rebecca was fired up, I was too, could we be falling in love? Or did we love each other already? These thoughts slipped from my mind as we kissed and caressed in the half light, our love making was tender until the end when it became furious. Spent, we lay on the bed I watched Rebecca smoke a cigarette, the smoke illuminated by the light from the hall swirling up towards the ceiling, the was a moist shine of sweat on her face, she looked magnificent to me; there was no need to say anything. At around two we went into the kitchen to make some coffee, we kissed again acknowledging in our way, that we had crossed a line, wherever it might take us, this was for real.

We did not need to talk about commitment each in our own way knew the responsibility we had taken on by making love, for me I would cherish this night like no other, I guessed Rebecca felt the same.

Chapter 6

January 1st to June 30th 2016

The ensuing months brought happiness that had seemed impossible in December just six months ago when we first met; now we were a couple and flitted to and fro between our respective homes as our love blossomed. I had settled into my job at Berkshire Developments and Charlie had kindly agreed to take Jason on and to my surprise and delight Mary as well, though I had to share them with Bill Bradshaw, the senior Surveyor for BD. The main issue about the arguments between main contractor, sub-contractors and designers was the programming. Not only were the program times in my opinion far too short and ambitious, not allowing for proper drying out before finishes were applied but also because the programs did not fully identify mile stone key events in particular for Mechanical and Electrical services which were becoming more and more sophisticated to meet for ever changing IT requirements. I suggested to Charles that we produce a sample program which we wanted all contractors to use in future. The program was to include detailed design time and approvals for specialist services. At present the services would be shown as two bars first and second fix. The new program had a slot for individual service design and approvals. First and second fix and then importantly, program slots for inspection, testing and commissioning of services. All too often the main contractor would ring up the sub-contractor and say "I want your commissioning engineer down here tomorrow, the programs running late". and then ring again saying "Something has come up and the commissioning had to be delayed". All this confusion cost money and delays and led to arguments. The new program was developed to eliminate the arguments; subcontractors were when appointed were to complete their section of the program for the Main Contractors approval. It was seen as a big step forward by all parties and where there were delays the program had to be modified and reissued so each party including Berkshire Developments and all contractors knew what was happening, with the internet to hand modifications could be issued within hours rather than days. Charles was particularly pleased and said the board had agreed to my having twelve thousand, five hundred pounds being a quarter of my bonus for my contribution, it was thought the new procedures would improve performance and in the long run save them money and provided them with better constructed buildings. I was thrilled and it gave me the money I needed to spoil Rebecca, it did not bother me that she was vastly more wealthy than me but I wanted to stand my corner, now I could afford to take her to the best restaurants that she liked and purchase some items of jewellery that I wanted to buy, in particular a gold broach with three half carat diamonds across the bridge, it was a pretty thing and one night when we were having a meal in Kensington High Street I gave it to her, She blushed and a tear fell from her eye onto her cheek. "I don't deserve this," she said wiping the tear from her cheek. "That's why I wanted to give it to you Rebecca, because you weren't expecting it."

She reached across the table and squeezed my hand. "Wait until I get you home, you beautiful man."

I pretended to look around saying, "Who me?" There were so many wonderful times in the first six months of our love affair; I had become a new man, if you can understand. I don't believe in comparing one time with another or one lover with another but where as Jane and I had our moments she could be very stubborn like her mother and this lead to furious arguments. I had no doubt some of these were fuelled by her mother who wanted to see our marriage come to an end. Where Jane was concerned it had at times been war, whereas Rebecca and I seemed to fit like hand and glove. We had never argued we enjoyed pleasing one another more than pleasing ourselves; it seemed to me to be a perfect match, though of course there was always a space in my heart for Jane and the terrible suffering I witnessed as she fought to live but died in tremendous pain. Rebecca carried on her work as before but having purchased the land in Esher and obtained planning permission with my help, Richard had begun the build at the end of April. I had been engaged by his company to undertake the planning and building control submissions which were approved in principal by the end of March. I also prepared and co-ordinated the services drawings for Richard, no mean feat, but it was essential that all the services were properly co-ordinated if they were to function properly. The gas boiler and principal electrical supply were housed in the cellar. The foundations and over site concrete had been laid and over seen by Walter Smith and the shape of the house was taking place, Rebecca had put her flat up for sale and we agreed that should the sale proceed quickly ahead of the completion of the new house she could live with me or rent on a short lease until the house in Esher was ready for occupation. We were blissfully happy and had spent a few days in Northumberland visiting Sea Houses, Bamburgh Castle and Holy Island, Northumberland is one of the most magical and romantic places in England and an opportunity to give the Jag a real run out, it coped beautifully with everything we threw at it, Rebecca insisted on doing most of the driving, it was great fun. We were sorry to have to make our way back to Kensington; it had been a busy time with plenty more to come. It was flaming June and the temperature was in the eighties. It was a Friday and I was in Manchester when Rebecca at home received a call from Norman Broadbent, she was in the living room ironing and watching the TV when the phone rang.

"Hello darlin, how's me little Becky then?"

Rebecca was stunned by the familiarity of the voice; she recognised the voice as someone she knew, but could not put a name to it.

"Who is this please?" She said with some alarm, the voice sounded ingratiating "It's Norm me auld mocker, Norman Broadbent, surely you remember me Becky?"

Rebecca cast her mind back twenty years, she remembered Norman Broadbent was the roadie for the group 'A Paler Shade of Blue' a nasty piece of work if she remembered correctly.

"What do you want Norman?" she asked politely.

"Now, now then Becky, you sound disappointed to ear from me darlin, I fourt you'd be appy to hear from a long lost pal from the past, oo's fallin on ard times."

"What is it you want Norman?" She sensed it was money; he was tapping up people he had worked with in the past, he wanted money.

"Well as you're askin, which is kind and foughtful of you Beck, me ole vans gone kaput, n-gins clapped out, en I need me van for me work, light removals these days."

"I'm not a mechanic Norman, sorry I can't help there."

"No but you have plenty of dosh, and been see in that fancy house they're buildin in Esher is yours, must be costing you a pretty penny.

"I don't see it as any of your business Norman, now if you don't mind I am busy."

"Not so fast darlin, I wasn't asking you to give me muney fer nuffin; I wouldn't do that to a good friend like you. No Becky, I ave sum fink to sell, sum fin I fink you will wana to buy."

"I'm not with you Norman, what would I want to buy from you?" Rebecca was trying to establish where the conversation was going.

"You remember Stew Walker, guitar player, you ad a fling with im, if I remember."

"If you say so Norman but I fail to see what business it is of yours and it was over twenty years ago, what are you trying to say?"

"Well Beck, sum photos of you and Stew have surfaced so's to speak, bit spicy if I might say, even for me en my tastes. As a good friend I didn't want them getting into the rong hands so to speak, so I'v given you ferst shot, got newspapers men, sniffin arand. Can't be fairer than that, can I me old mocker."

The pieces fell into shape; Stewart Walker was part of the jazz group she had belonged to. 'A Paler Shade of Blue' for three stormy years she had been the lead singer until she nearly died of a drug overdose. In those days pretty much anything and everything happened, she had been to bed with three of the five man group over the years, none of the flings lasted or mattered, other than with Chas, it was just a way of life. After rehab she spent a year at college studying accountancy and began slowly to rebuild her life. She lost touch with the members of the group, if she remembered correctly Norman was their roadie, a dower gaunt faced cockney, five eight, thin as a rake, wiry but strong as an ox, a friend of Chas French who had formed the group, Norman looked like a ferret, he certainly behaved like an animal, usually unshaven, brown teeth, through chain smoking, and wore those horrible fingerless mittens, which were even worn when eating, it was revolting. Norman wanted to be in the band but couldn't sing for toffee, had no understanding of jazz, couldn't play a musical instrument and was ugly to boot.

"Are you still there Becky?" she heard Norman asking down the phone. "How many photos are there Norman?"

"Five, A4 size, nice close up pics of you en stew havin it off, a couple of explicit ones if I may say, you ad a nice bum in those days."

"Don't be vulgar Norman, how much?" the penny had dropped, she was being blackmailed. "I fourt a grand a pic is more van fair, Star and Sun would pay me double, but I don't want to see me old mocker dragged through the dert and spoilin her career and relationship with that fancy bloke you hav in tow."

"I can't get my hands on that amount of money just like that Norman."

"Okay Becky, I ring you tomorrow but don't think you can muck me abart darlin or you'd be readin abart yer self in the Fleet Street rags with a picture of your bum on page three. The thought made Rebecca cringe. Norman rang off and Rebecca found herself rushing to the toilet where she was violently sick. She staggered into the bedroom her head throbbing and sweat pouring off her. She took her clothes off and went to the bathroom where she showered. Calming down she made some tea but decided a brandy was what she needed she poured about five fingers into a tumbler and laying on the bed, tried to think what to do For some reason she was less concerned as to what I might say than the impact it would have on her career and where she worked, and the new house, what would the neighbours think? It made her shudder as she took a large pull on the brandy. After an hour or so of running the alternatives around in her head she decided to tell me. She rang my mobile and I confirmed I would be catching the four thirty train from Manchester Piccadilly and would be home about seven; I sensed something was wrong but when I asked she said she would, tell me when I got home. I wondered what was troubling Rebecca it was not like her to phone during the day, so it must be something serious. I wrote up my notes on Eastleigh an M&E contractor as something to do and give me some time in the morning. I had a bad feeling about the phone call, but it would have to wait until I got home. When I got home Rebecca fell in to my arms sobbing. It took a while for her to calm down and tell me about the phone call from Norman Broadbent. She was right in telling me, though it took a while, she was crying and drinking to keep calm. I had never been judgemental where people's personal lives were concerned. And when I said it was not my business what she did twenty years ago I felt the palpable relief in her voice and manner. We discussed the options I asked if she knew where he lived she said she had goggled Norman Broadbent and it came up with an address in North Harrow a breakers yard. She didn't seem to think he was worried about her knowing where he lived, he had been very clever on the phone to stress he was trying to help her.

"I might pay him a visit and break his legs."

"That's not like you David," she said adding, "I didn't know you were potentially violent, I agree with your sentiment but it won't help me."

"No," I said reluctantly, "I didn't know I could become violent either but if this man Norman Broadbent hurts you, he's a dead man walking."

"David," she exclaimed.

"I mean it Rebecca, if he hurts you," I let the words hang in the air. In the end we decided that I would hand over the money and making it clear what the consequences were if he came back for more or went to the press. Not surprisingly Norman didn't like the idea of my handing him the money but reluctantly agreed when Rebecca explained that she could not be seen withdrawing five thousand pounds from her bank when her job was auditing the movement of money and was audited herself by the company she worked for. It was a moot point and one Norman had not thought about when he phoned her again. She explained that if wanted the money my giving him the money was the only option. He agreed but wanted a further thousand, it was his way of saying I'm in charge. They agreed that I would hand over the money in the pub opposite the breakers yard on Friday night at six o'clock. I didn't tell Rebecca what I had in mind but it wasn't pretty. I went over to the wardrobe and from behind a cardboard box where I kept spare shoes I took out a small hardwood chest. Inside was one of my father's guns which I had discovered when I was clearing out the house following his death. He was a keen shot and belonged to a shooting the Croydon Rifle and Pistol Club. After my fathers funeral I had returned all the guns into the police or I thought I had, this one I discovered later, came in a beautiful veneered box, locked with a brass key and a note inside from my father. '*Keep this one David you never know if you may need to use it.*' So I was in possession of an un-licensed 9mm Glock, silencer and bullets in pristine condition. I had never like guns or the thought of owning one or heaven forbid using one, until now it hadn't been in my nature. I took the gun out of the box, checked it was loaded and put it in the deep pocked of my coat. At four o'clock I went to the bank and withdraw six thousand pounds in twenty pound notes from my savings account. I had a feeling I was being watched and had Jason standing on the opposite side of the road, waiting to see if I was being watched. He noticed one person loitering around in front of the bank. Norman was unaware we were surveying him whilst he surveyed me. Jason was able to take a photograph of Norman from his mobile phone, which was to prove invaluable when I met up with him later. I looked at the photo of Norman Broadbent he was a thin wiry man with a sallow face and heavy growth of hair around his face, he looked menacing with two day stubble. He wore a long black leather coat, the type you see when cowboys ride into town in American westerns with a wide brimmed black leather hat and black boots. In the photo Jason gave me, Norman was smoking a cigarette; if you likened him to an animal I guess you would have to say he looked like a ferret or a rodent of some kind. Then at six o'clock, looking at the breakers yard opposite as I walked over to the pub I was sure Norman lived in squalor, drinking mugs of tea laced with whiskey, out of dirty unwashed mugs. Time would tell, I walked into the pub ordered a pint of bitter and walked the length of the main bar and sat in a corner my back to the wall. I didn't have to wait long, A young man twenty six or twenty seven years old, about six foot six, eighteen stone with a Slavic, east European looking face walked up to me, he was dressed in a black tea shirt which proudly sported the warning in gold letters 'Don't mess with me' and dirty faded jeans. His shaven head added to the look of menace He walked straight up to me and said,

"Mr Rogan, the money, and then you get the photos." I looked at his hard ugly face, it wasn't Normans.

"I came to see Norman Broadbent, what's your game Ivan?" I said, he looked startled.

"My names is Ivan, how did you know my name? Anyway Normans not available, you give me the money Mr Rogan." He held out his hand.

I looked at Ivan and said, "Ivan if you know what's good for you sit down and listen, I have a Glock in my right hand pointed at the space just above where your legs join up, in case you are not familiar with English Ivan, a Glock is a gun, don't make me pull the trigger." He looked under the table.

"You wouldn't dare, in a place like this it's full of people."

"I would Ivan, it's fitted with a silencer." I pulled the gun from under the table and told him to be a good boy and sit down. I watched his eyes revolving around their sockets as he tried to work out what he should do next, sensible boy, he sat down.

"Now put the photos on the table along with your wallet, car keys and your mobile phone, his clenched fists were the size of saucers."

His face was glowing a deep red colour as he tried to control his temper.

"Now take out the photos and tear them up and put the bits of paper back in the envelope and phone your boss, tell him there's a bit of a complication and can he come over." He gave me a filthy look.

"You'll regret this Mr Rogan."

And then Ivan picked up the phone and called Norman, saying, "It's Ivan boss, Rogan's got the money but insists on seeing you."

He put the phone down. I passed him some cheap hand cuffs I had purchased and told him to put them on reminding him the gun was still pointing towards his private parts.

"If we meet again mister I'll tear your head off."

"I don't see that we will ever meet again Ivan, you have just become a liability to Norman Broadbent, I would scarper if I were you."

He sat moodily as Norman walked up.

"Spotted me little rouses then Mr Rogan."

He said sitting down, "Where the money?"

In my holdall, Norman, now tell your Russian Rottweiler to take a walk."

"What is this?" Norman said looking at Ivan. Before Ivan could reply my gun appeared above the table.

"Are you mad or somefin?" Norman said stubbing out his cigarette on the table leg.

"No not at all Norman just going through the motions of another day at the office." I looked at Ivan seeing he was going to lunge at me so I shot him aiming for his hands, the gun made a soft popping sound as the bullet penetrated his right hand.

"Time to leave Ivan." He went to pick up his stuff he had left on the table.

"You can leave your stuff on the table Ivan, and if I see you again, the next bullet will be in your forehead. I wanted to teach him a lesson, I watched him get up and pushing the chair to one side with his cuffed hands left through the back entrance that led to the car park. I turned to face Norman.

"Your turn Norman, empty your pockets and don't do anything silly."

I could see he was furious, with Ivan as well as me; he put a shabby black wallet on the table bulging with what looked like twenty and fifty pound notes, some loose change, car keys and another bunch of keys which I guessed were to the Yard and flat over, the mobile was a small Nokia.

"Now that was easy, Norman, I am going to ask you a couple of questions and I know it's difficult for a serial liar but I want you to be honest with me."

There was a look of confusion on his face. I put all the items on the table into the grey holdall I had brought with me and contained the six thousand pounds which I showed him his eyes gleamed as he saw the money.

"There's still a chance you will get your money Norman; it depends on how truthful you are, okay." He nodded;

"I don't believe the set of photos you gave Ivan to give me are the only copy, I need to know how many copies there are and who has them if its not you."

He looked at me again with a troubled face, lighting another cigarette, the bar man came over wagging a finger and told him to put it out. Norman stamped it out on the floor and lit another one as soon as the barman turned and walked away and was about to speak but before he could reply I said.

"The truth Norman you saw what happened to Ivan, it wont be as pleasant for you, a bullet in the guts put an end to your stud duties and ruin your leather coat as well."

I watched him flinch at the thought of a bullet in the guts.

"I've only the one copy, Ray Guest has the originals he was a member of the group, drummer, ugly git, the only one that Becky didn't do it with, eld a grudge."

"Where does he live Norman?"

"Am Common, got a nice drum out there, wife en two kids."

"Will he be in?"

"What now?"

"Yeah, now Norman."

I gave Norman his phone and he rang Ray who confirmed he was in, Norman said he had the money and wanted to drop over.

I could hear Ray's reply.

"Yeah come on over Norm, wife and kids are out, have a couple of beers and plan our next line of attack, twenty big ones next time, bleed the bitch dry. Norman closed the call saying he would be about thirty minutes and handed me the phone and I said,

"Now we are going to leave Norman and pay Ray a little visit, I am afraid you will be in the boot of the car but I will try to avoid the pot holes, come on and if you play your cards right I'll give you whatever Ray was going to give you for helping Rebecca, as you put it."

Norman looked small and defeated as he got up and we made our way to the car park, I had parked up at five. I lifted the boot up; the pub car park was empty and I pushed Norman into the boot and taping his mouth with duct tape and tying his hands set off for the address he had given me. With the sat nav it was easy to find Ray's house which was set back on a well to do road, must be worth a few bob, I thought. I opened the boot briefly to let some air in and told Norman I wouldn't be long and provided everything went alright would have him back at North Harrow by nine clock, ready for a pint and his pay off and closed the boot lid. I walked up to the front door and knocked. The door opened and a man about my age in shorts, sweater and sandals and large sun glasses, opened the door.

"Sorry mate don't buy anything from cold callers."

He went to close the door; I pushed the door back towards him and showed him the gun.

"Norman sent me."

He looked confused. "Norman who? What's your game mate?"

"Norman Broadbent sent me to pick up your copy of the original photos of Stew and Becky. Said his life depended on it."

Wayne looked at me again more confused as he closed the door and we walked into the large living room.

"Sit-down Ray," I said, "and hand me your wallet, mobile phone car and house keys." I don't know why but he obeyed me without comment.

"Now the photos." He said they were in his study, so I said ok, we would go together and get them, he asked where Norman was, I told him Norman had had a spot of bother and his muscle Ivan had hurt his hand.

"I find the gun comes in handy, when people get silly."

I smiled as we made our way to the study; he gave me a large envelope which contained seven photos. "Are you sure these are the only copies."

He nodded and looked like a frightened rabbit. We walked back down stairs and back into the lifting room.

"I couldn't help hearing of your latest little caper to bleed Rebecca of another twenty grand."

He looked at me petrified, as I waved the gun side ways in front of him. "No never was going to happen, my silly joke."

"Yeah," I said, mimicking him, I took the photos out of the envelope and tore them up and put the pieces of paper back into the envelope.

"You sure these are the only copies?"

"Yeah they are the only copy."

"See it would be a shame if I had to come back what with your wife and kids at home, it's so easy for people to get caught in the cross fire when people misunderstand each other especially when I have the keys to your house."

I paused for a moment then said smiling.

"I find this difficult but I have to hurt you sufficiently for you to fully understand." I didn't need to go any further the was a sudden bowl movement and the stench of human waste as I shot his little finger off his left hand, I presumed he was right handed. I picked up his keys, wallet and mobile phone and let myself out, what to do about Norman, he was made of sterner stuff than poor old Ray, I wondered what he would say to his wife when she returned with the kids from the gym, I drove to Gatwick airport and parked up in the long stay car park and opened the boot and let a relieved Norman out, he wobbled for a moment as I untied him and removed the duct tape.

"I think we understand each other Norman. If I see your ugly face again, I will shoot you, Ray's got the message and I am sorry I have broken my word but I've decided you are not getting any money either. Don't like giving back word but there you are, remember I have your house and car keys and now I know what you look like, probably time for you to move on."

I got in the car and drove off, knowing Norman was clever enough to get a lift and find his way back home. Of course, one can never be sure but I didn't think Rebecca would be troubled by Ray and Norman again.

I had left Norman to fend for himself; I was reasonably confident he would find his way home and learned not to tangle with me in the future. The way I saw it was that Ray had used Norman to get at Rebecca. Now Ray was much older, close to drawing his pension, married and had two children he had more to lose now he had been found out certainly as much as Rebecca and now he knew I was on the case I would be surprised if he pushed the matter further. If Norman was sensible he would take his cue from Ray and slide back into the woodwork. When I got home Rebecca looked pensive expecting the worst. I said I couldn't guarantee that the issue was dead in the water but I would be surprised if we heard from Norman again.

I didn't go into the details or let her know that I had shot Ivan through the palm of his hand in a pub in North Harrow and shot Ray's little finger off his left hand so he would remember to leave you alone and cut a jagged cross on the right hand side of Norman's left cheek, a nice timely reminder to behave himself when he looked in the mirror. If there was going to be a fly in the ointment it was Ivan, he was the sort of man that bore a grudge. I would let the authorities know there was an illegal immigrant working for Norman. Hopefully Ivan would get deported but I needed to keep tabs on Ivan. We had chicken with a pepper sauce new potatoes and peas accompanied by a white wine. I felt quite pleased with myself and said to Rebecca that the trick was to make the blackmailer as fearful of the consequences as his victim. I also realised just how much I loved Rebecca and would go further if they started again, being a criminal didn't seem to bother me. All Rebecca knew was that there had been a confrontation in which Ivan, Norman and Ray had come a poor second. I mentioned that Ray had planned to increase the cost photos to twenty grand after the first payment so we could never be sure. She was still shivering when we went to bed.

Chapter 7

July to December 31st 2016

The whole incident of the abortive blackmail instigated by Norman Broadbent and Ray Guest had a demoralising effect on Rebecca; somehow it had put her on the back foot. I guessed she had lost some of her confidence, that the episode was pulling her back into her past. Whatever it was she never spoke about it. I sensed that unless invited this was not an issue for me to pursue. So I kept to what I did best, which was being patient, I felt sure an opportunity would arise when she would confide in me. In the meantime there was plenty to keep both of us busy with the house build project but it was a quite time for both of us. One day in August we were having dinner at my flat, Chicken and chips this time, there was no end to my cooking skills, I even managed not to over cook the frozen peas and cheated with the pepper sauce which I purchased ready made from Waitrose. I had got used to Rebecca's quite moods but this evening she seemed brighter and had her blue dress on, the one she wore last year to Charlie Patterson's charity dinner at Claridge's.

"I like the dress."

I said as I came in with the chicken ready served up on the plates. "Shall I pour she said picking up the bottle of wine, she poured two generous measures and we toasted each other before starting on the chicken.

"You're getting quite good at this David," she was smiling, something which she rarely did these days.

"I have a good teacher," I said by way of reply.

"I spoke to Richard today, all things being well the house should be finished and ready to move in by the end of November, ready for Christmas."

"That's great news Rebecca."

"Are you still game to move in with me?"

"Nothing in the world would stop me Rebecca, you know that."

"You might change your mind when I ask you my next request."

"I doubt that."

"David, I have been unwell for some time, since that unfortunate business with Norman Broadbent and the odious Ray Guest, but I hope I am getting through it, in any event, would you be so kind as to marry me?"

"I was gob smacked; I saw her face flush red, as she said. "Hurry up the chickens getting cold."

I stood up and went around to her side and kissed her passionately as she looked up at me with here moist amber eyes.

"It would be the greatest honour of my life Rebecca, I would have asked myself but I know you've been unwell."

"Good that's settled she said as I returned to my chair. We can get married at Chelsea Registry office, sometime in October I think; we'll have a quiet wedding."

"You've been planning this, what has brought this about?" I said smiling.

"Oh, I don't know, I am looking forward to living in the new house and if we live in it together I want us to be married, I can't tell you exactly why, other than I love you as much as I did when we first met."

"Tomorrow I'll put my flat up for sale and we are off to Bond Street, I want to buy my fiancée her engagement ring."

There was a little tear and then she smiled again looking radiant, the first time for several weeks but I knew no more about her past than I did before, but I guessed it must have been something dreadful. The days and weeks passed in a bit of a blur, I was still busy at work whilst Rebecca when she was well enough over saw the work at the house and arranged the wedding details, her moods were up and down, her doctor had prescribed anti depressants' but I thought they made things worse not better but I didn't say. She had asked and been given a year off work, giving health issues as the reason. Rebecca was highly thought of at Parsons, Patterson and Peters the auditors and the senior partner readily agreed, saying the job would always be there when she wanted it and was fit enough to return. In truth James Peters was getting on and knew it wouldn't be long before the two other partners suggested he retire, Rebecca was the obvious choice to become the third partner, something James Peters would not kindly agree to, though that decision would not be his to take, so he was pleased that Rebecca would be out of the game for a year. It wasn't that he didn't like her, what was there to dislike, it was that she was too damn clever, more suited to running his side of the business than he was, he detested career women, however good. Had the other partners known of James Peters thoughts, he would have been out, there was no place for grace and favour at PPP, but they didn't know and Rebecca was only pleased to have been granted some breathing space for her fragile health to recover.

Our civil wedding in October was a very quiet affair, when I asked her if anyone was coming from her side, she said just two friends, there wasn't anyone and I didn't ask. The wedding was attended by Charles and Betty Patterson who were witnesses to the marriage, Jason and his partner Sally, Mary Wiltshire Dawn Rogers, James Peters and his wife Grace and two women from PPP that Rebecca had known for many years and Richard and Barbara Brown. After the short registry office service, we made our way to a bistro in Fulham that Rebecca liked for our wedding breakfast although it was three o'clock by the time we arrived, we had a small room to ourselves, it was an intimate affaire, quiet and dignified, I think everyone knew that Rebecca had not been well. We didn't have a honeymoon as such but returned to my flat, I could tell that the whole experience whilst wonderful had taken a lot out of Rebecca, though she would never have admitted it. The flat sold within the first week and subject to our house being ready on the seventeenth of November we would move out of my flat and into the new house, I couldn't wait though in reality we had only enough furniture to fill half the house, two of the bedrooms would remain empty for a while. The only snag we had was with the landlines and internet connection but after someone from BT came round, it got sorted; we were on super fast fibre broadband apparently. There wasn't a day when I didn't have reason to be concerned over Rebecca's health and with Charlie's blessing I took some extended leave. It was the third week in October there was much to do and Rebecca was too unwell to do very much. Most days she slept until ten thirty or so, when she asked if I was disappointed or angry with her I would kiss her and tell her how much I loved her, something from her past was dragging her down and at the moment she did not have the strength to fight it off.

We moved in over the third weekend of November, the last warm weekend before winter set in, it was like everything we did these days quiet though Rebecca seemed excited when we sat down to lunch. Grilled salmon this time I was branching out, cooked in our new kitchen and eaten in the small dining area to the side of it. We had advertised for a house keeper and gardener come handyman and three days after we moved in there was a knock at the door. I opened the door to see a rather petite looking woman standing in the door way, I would say in her forties standing on the steps, she bowed slowly saying she was Bella Rodriguez and had come in respect of the advertisement for a cook and house keeper, she had what I thought was a nice disposition, it was in her eyes, they were warm enquiring and inviting. I asked her to come in as a head popped up from above the hedge at the front of the house. She turned around.

"This is my husband Pedro, he is rather shy, however he is a keen gardener and also a good handyman, you will like." Bella added, "Pedro doesn't speak English."

She beckoned Pedro to come over and like Bella; Pedro bowed as he took my hand, and gave me a limp handshake.

"You had better come in, I took them into the reception room whilst I went to look for Rebecca, thankfully she was up and came down the stairs as I was going to go up.

"We have visitors, Rebecca."

"I see," she said kissing me swiftly on the cheek; we entered the reception room together.

"This is my wife Rebecca she is the mistress of this house and this is Bella and Pedro Rodriguez, they have come about the position of cook, house keeper and handy man."

"They are married Rebecca," I said with amusement. The pleasantries took place whilst I went to make some coffee, when I returned I noticed that Rebecca had changed her seat and was now sitting beside Bella, they were engaged in conversation, Bella looked up taking the coffee cup from me.

"We have been talking Senor David; your wife is very beautiful."

I smiled this was going to be a very unusual interview, I sat down beside Pedro and we both listened as the women continued their conversation."

"Do you want to show Pedro around the garden and the rest of the house David?" Rebecca enquired; we took the hint and made our way through the lounge which led to the utility room which in turn led to the rear garden. Pedro was as big as Bella was small, but he wasn't tall, he had a typical Spanish stocky look, five seven, one sixty pounds, sun browned skin, a thin nose, raven black hair, a hang dog moustache, he was casually dressed I guessed about forty, he looked younger than his wife and a little like a Mexican bandit you see in Cowboy films. I led him to the greenhouse first and he exclaimed in broken English how wonderful it was, he liked the garden space very much although it needed a lot of work in the coming months, I asked if they had a car, "A small VW," Pedro replied sheepishly.

"Did he know much about cars?"

"Some," he replied.

"What about the gas boiler and the electrics?" I asked.

"Some," he replied again. He certainly was a man of few words, when we got back to the reception room it was empty, Rebecca was showing Bella the kitchen and utility rooms.

"I love the pantry Senor David, you have a very beautiful house, who ever designed it was a gifted man."

"That's yours truly," Rebecca said to Bella, "My husband, David designed this house."

As it happened Bella and Pedro Rodriguez spent most of the

afternoon with us. I could tell Rebecca was impressed by the way Bella spoke about how she would look after the house and what Pedro's duties would entail, it was clear who was in the driving seat and it wasn't Pedro. Whilst the two women were dotting the I's and crossing the T's I was showing Pedro my wood turning lathe. The outcome of it all was that subject to the references being acceptable Bella and her husband would start their duties on the sixth of December.

"What a way to finish the year," Rebecca said after they had left. It was clear they got on.

"Thank you David for giving me free rein with the interview, Bella is of the old school which suits me perfectly." I wasn't sure what she meant by this, but if Rebecca was happy! So was I after a fashion, I can't tell you what it was, what made me feel a little uneasy, but I felt something was not right, I had no idea what and let my thoughts hang in the air, Rebecca would have been mortified if I mentioned my unease. The reference from a Mrs Fielding who had lived in a large house in Dulwich confirmed that Bella and her husband Pedro Rodriguez were who they said they were. Mrs Fielding had finally come to terms with moving into a care home due to various illnesses but her mind was as sharp as a knife and she spoke highly of Bella and her husband Pedro who she said made her laugh. That was good enough for Rebecca. I hoped that this was the beginning of Rebecca's recovery for the following days, her well being picked up and she was doing things again but her moods were still up and down and unpredictable. What was encouraging was Bella's infinite patience, I knew when Rebecca was struggling and did my best to support her.

Bella had agreed with Rebecca that she could bring some of her possessions to the flat when they moved in which included cutlery and crockery they had inherited from Pedro's mother and an old rocking chair, dining room table and chairs Pedro had made, when they first got married, although Rebecca was getting better or so I hoped she was too ill to attend Charlie Patterson's 'Save the children' do, so we cried off with Charlie's blessing having paid the mandatory twelve hundred pounds for two tickets and a donation of five thousand pounds. Having sold both houses we were comfortably well off and had no need to worry about money or income for the foreseeable future. It wouldn't have mattered whether we had any money or not I was not going to leave Rebecca alone and between us someone was with Rebecca most of the time she was not sleeping. It was a big worry made so much more bearable by Bella's constant attention to Rebecca's welfare, she was truly a marvel.

Christmas and the New Year were quiet affairs, of course Bella and Pedro were excited and they joined us for Christmas dinner and the New Year dinner and we exchanged small Christmas presents. We had crossed the line between being employer and employed but I could see this was mainly of Rebecca's making.

Anyone could see Bella adored Rebecca like a daughter adored its mother. It was I believed good for Rebecca and took a lot of worry off my shoulders I lent Pedro one of my old DJs for the supper, it was quiet and in its way a charming evening, however as soon as it was twelve o'clock we both retired to bed.

The New Year brought change and bleak news for both of us.

Chapter 8
15th January 2017

Things were still good as we entered the second week in January, Rebecca was making plans for fitting out the empty guest rooms allowing Bella to join in the fun, it was wonderful to see her smiling and excited, there was a cold snap in the third week of January and we both sat and watched from the French windows as the snow, silently began to fall and drift into mounds, we spent most of the time sitting quietly in the dining room looking out to the back garden as the snow began to cover the ground and the sun house at the bottom of the garden. It had a magical effect on our senses transporting us to a tranquil place, of course once the snow turns to slush its not such a pretty sight but in its pristine condition the snow was breath taking, well we thought so anyway and most importantly Rebecca seemed to be getting better. The furniture schedule for three of the empty bedrooms had been chosen and we were going to place orders for the same at a local furniture shop the first week in February, sadly this was not to be. Four column inches on page two of the twenty fifth of Januarys 'Times' newspaper shattered the peacefulness, we were enjoying.

***Stewart Walker** a session musician and one time member of the jazz group 'A Paler Shade of Blue'*

was found dead at his home in Salisbury along with his wife Anne and two children. Josh aged seven and Belinda aged five. It is believed there was a gas explosion at the house. At this time the Police couldn't rule out foul play.

I would never have let Rebecca see the article but a supposed friend of hers, Joanne Wallis from PPP rang and asked her if she had heard the news.

Rebecca immediately sent Pedro to the local newsagents, requesting him too bring a copy of the Times back to the house. When I came home from having the company car pass its MOT, Bella came rushing up to me.

"Its Rebecca Senor David, she is in bed, she looks very pale as if she is in a state of shock."

I took the stairs two at a time as I ran quickly to her bedroom. Rebecca was lying peacefully on the bed; I noticed she was breathing, thank God. I took her hand and she opened her eyes, she looked as if she were in pain. "Are you okay?" I asked quietly.

She nodded and pointed to the paper lying folded at the bottom of the bed. It took me a minute to find the offending article, which was a dreadful thing to think, four people had lost their lives and all I could think was that it had upset my wife, no matter how crass that was; my only concern at the time was Rebecca. I could do nothing to bring Stewart Walker and his family back to life but I had to do something to assuage the waves of guilt and depression which I feared were rolling through Rebecca's mind. I squeezed her hand as Bella came in with some tea; we sat on the bed and comforted her as best we could. "What does it mean David, the police can't rule out foul play?

"It's only general police talk Rebecca, they can't rule out what they don't know at this time. They don't have any alternative than to say this if asked by a reporter."

"Oh," Rebecca said unconvinced.

"Drink some tea senora," Bella said handing her the cup. Rebecca took the tiniest of swallows and tried to smile, to tell us she was okay. Her doctor as before prescribed more powerful anti depressants and rest and not to let her see the papers or watch the television news, anything which might distress her, whilst her mind adjusted to the tragic news. The radio station played the bands signature tune 'A Paler Shade of Blue' as a tribute to Stewart Walker.

'A Paler Shade of Blue'

Words by Rebecca Davies, Music by Chas French/Stewart Walker

Your eyes, your eyes The colour of the skies

Are a paler shade of blue.

A paler shade of blue

The love that I once knew.

I knew, and I knew as I looked Into your eyes that love never Dies,
it might change colour, it Might as it hears you're wailful Cries,
the deepness of your sighs Reflecting in your eyes

A paler shade of blue.

I love you, I love you; I love you Because you're true

Because you're

A paler shade of blue

Rebecca's plaintive voice rapt around Stewarts saxophone and Chas's electric guitar and Allen Fender, harmonic keyboards filled the room with the sound of raw anguish, hope, love lost and found, Rebecca had a unique voice that was able to bend, stretch and elongate words and sounds, to give them depth and in some cases new meaning. She was good but anyone in the music industry knew it could not last; no one could perform at that level, in that way day after day without burning themselves out,

England's Billy Holiday, a shining star. That's what I believed happened to her twenty years ago. Bella seemed mesmerised; there were tears in her eyes.

"That's you Senora I heard your song on the radio this morning, what a beautiful voice you have."

"Had, Bella, had."

I guessed any number of memories would be flashing through her mind, there was not much either Bella or myself could do other than be attentive, Rebecca's smile was weak and she looked very tired. The words of that song hung in my mind, I imagined her singing 'A Paler Shade of Blue' in a sleazy night club in Falmouth or St Ives, wearing her skimpy white dress, bare footed, the look of a frightened bird on her face in between tearful smiles the audience in raptures. The bedroom was silent, no one spoke. Rebecca tried to speak but could not find the energy to describe the memories flooding her mind, instead she lay still she found herself taken back some twenty years ago into a past where she hardly recognised herself, it was a life time ago and she was a different person. A picture of Stewart Walker formed in her mind. He was easily the best musician of the oddly formed band, and very accomplished, playing keyboards, Guitar, piano and saxophone, he doubled up with Chas on the backing vocals and wrote some of the bands best songs along with Rebecca. Stewart was rather short, five seven and slim build with a flush of mousey blonde hair hanging down to his shoulders, He wore an old leather bomber jacket over a pale blue shirt and jeans, apart from his musical talents she remembered his hair and delicate hands were his best features. He didn't have the looks, wit or charm of Chas French but Stewart had presence, brought to the fore by his playing ability. She recalled the song that had made him and her briefly famous. 'Thelma'. She gripped her hands together as she sang the words quietly to herself, in those brief moments she was seventeen again and on stage with Stewart somewhere in Falmouth performing the song 'Thelma' to rapturous applause.

'Thelma'
Words and Music by Stewart Walker

When I'm at home Or all alone

And cannot sleep

I play my saxophone She makes me weep It's a Stelma

And when I hold her She feels like a woman, I call her Thelma

Miss Moody and Blue She has the sweetest tone.

Long into the night we play Sometimes I let her stay Two lovers making music Until dawn and day light The start of another day.

If I were blind

I would not mind

For I can always find

Thelma in my mind

As she recalled the words and simple melody, a tear ran down her face followed by a fond smile. Rebecca and Stewart were never lovers as such; the first time was one night when they were all smashed, Allan Fender was the worst and most dangerous member of the band, when he had mixed cocaine and alcohol together. He had brutally bedded Rebecca one night bruising her and hitting her when she protested, it was nothing less than rape, in the morning when she challenged him, he shrugged his shoulders saying he couldn't remember, the truth was he couldn't care less. Then one night Rebecca recalled Allan coming in to her room in a filthy mood and was about to set about her when

Stewart came in, he saw the signs on Allan's face and quickly said to Allen that he and Rebecca were spending the night together and Cindy one of Allan's groupies was outside wanting to know if he wanted company. For once Allan had been out- witted and had walked away in a huff with the customary shrug of the shoulders, Rebecca remembered saying to Stewart at the time that he had probably saved her life. There were more brother and sister than lovers though Rebecca was sure they had made love at some time and from then on Allen left her alone. The chemistry between Rebecca and Stewart was never more noticeable than when they performed 'Thelma' together, just her singing and Stewart on the saxophone and one small spotlight spilling light on the floor in front of them, it was usually the last song of the gig, it was the last song on the first album.

Like Rebecca, Stewart didn't miss the band when they broke up after Rebecca had walked out or run away, they never got to the bottom of it. Stewart got a job at a college in Salisbury teaching music, bought a nice house with the proceeds of his time with the band, married a woman unconnected to the music industry and later they had two children. Rebecca wasn't to know that Norman Broadbent had made contact with Stewart, asking if he had any old photos of the group some twenty years later, saying he had clients who would pay big money for photos, the saucier the better. Stewart had never liked Norman and gave him short shrift. It wasn't until Stewart received a second call from Norman asking if he had changed his mind that he became suspicious and made the mistake of ringing Ray Guest to enquire if Norman had been pestering him as well, suggesting Norman should be reported to the police.

Things should have stopped there but the abortive blackmail attempt would lead the police straight to them if Stewart did report Norman to the police. Stewart had inadvertently signed his own death warrant, the plan had been to scare him off, not kill him and his family. He had always taken his wife and children to the cinema on a Friday night. On the night of the explosion they had returned home early, with their youngest boy David being sick. Norman was philosophical saying to Ray over the phone.

"Sorry mate, vees fings appen. Ray wasn't quite as nonchalant as Norman; it had been his idea to give Stewart a little warning, now he was a multi murderer. There was no turning back, getting rid of Rebecca followed by her new husband David Rogan was now a priority, as any time Rebecca might put two and two together following Stewart's death and the plan to relieve Rebecca of her money. By late afternoon a small group of reporters stood in the road, deciding who was going to venture up the path and presumably request an interview, I counted ten people milling around. We made some tea and Bella and I took them out to the waiting journalists.

"Good afternoon ladies and gentlemen, I have bought you all something to drink on this cold day, I must advise that my wife Rebecca is unwell and has been for some time. The news of Stewart Walker's death and that of his family has only made Rebecca's condition worse. She is not well enough to give an interview, the events you may want to write about occurred twenty years ago when she was little more than a girl in the company and working with men twice her age or more."

The journalists in the main respected my request and began to leave much to my relief. As soon as we were back inside Bella went and sat with Rebecca for some reason I went into the front reception room and walked over to the window and looked out. The snow had gone just as I was about to close the curtains something moved to my right it was someone surveying the house. I stopped dead still and continued looking out of the corner of my eye, whoever it was, I guessed it was a man, was huge, I thought for a moment. I was pretty sure it was Ivan lurking around outside the house. If it was him, I could only guess what he wanted. I moved slowly away from the window and went quickly to my study and found the Glock at the bottom of my sock drawer, checked it was loaded and went upstairs and told Bella we might have an unwanted visitor not to go out or open the doors to anyone she was to tell Pedro and not to tell or worry Rebecca. I then spent sometime thinking where Ivan might hide, if he was to break in, I figured it would be at night, so where would he hide? Either the greenhouse or the summer house. I explained to Rebecca I would be out for a while and carefully checking the greenhouse made myself as comfortable as I could, of course I could be completely wrong and he might break in from the front but the back was favourite mainly because he would not be seen from the road. If he was coming from the back or the summer house he would have to pass the greenhouse and I would be waiting. It was a long wait but at half past two in the morning, there was little light and no moon, I heard a noise. I couched down as the shadow of someone passed by. I watched Ivan pause by the kitchen window, dressed in a black jumper, black jeans and black trainers, he was wearing a balaclava, but I knew it was him, his huge hands were the give away, I knew if he hit me or got his hands around my neck I was a dead man. He was looking up I guess to see if he could climb on to the garage roof and from there into one of the unoccupied rear bedrooms. I took the gun from my waistband and repositioned myself by the corner of the greenhouse as he began to climb on to the garage roof using a wheely bin to gain leverage and extra height. I came up behind him as he was about to haul himself over the protruding garage fascia and gutter and on to the slopping roof above. That same feeling came over me as it had when I first encountered Ivan, I knew that carrying a gun and wanting to shoot someone was wrong, but it was swept aside by a more powerful force, the will to confront someone I considered was an enemy of Rebecca.

"Ivan," I said "What do you think you are doing?"

He looked around bearing his teeth, I had seen Rottweiler's before but none as grotesque and fearsome as Ivan in the human form, there were no second chances I fired into Ivan's left buttock and he gave a yelp. to make sure I had the upper hand I fired again into his right buttock he gave another yelp as the wheelie bin moved sideways as he tried in vain to regain his footing, firing his own gun wildly, he fell heavily to the ground. He managed to get up and stared at me with a look of hatred in his eyes, I stood motionless, the gun pointing at him.

"I kill you," he roared and lunged forwards towards me firing his gun but the bullets harmlessly hit the pathway instead of me, I fired again and this time he was facing me and I couldn't miss though it took three more rounds before he fell at my feet. In a state of shock, I called the police and then the ambulance though this only so they could bring the body bag. Ivan was dead; I had killed a man and was relieved and pleased rather than grieved and full of remorse. Of course, Rebecca would be furious but she had not had to deal with him he was a monster and would have torn me limb from limb had he got hold of me. When I finally went upstairs to see Rebecca it was seven in the morning. I expected Rebecca to be asleep but she was wide awake talking to Bella. I marvelled at Bella patience and said. Why don't you go to bed and get some sleep Bella?"

"No!" she replied. "It's no hardship but a pleasure to care for my mistress."

I was not sure how much detail to go into but I explained that man who I had shot was the same man who had tried to take the money at the pub in North Harrow and I believed he was going to break in to our home mainly because I had seen through him and when he went for me had shot Ivan in the hand. Rebecca looked alarmed, tired and pale.

"How will it all end David?" She asked, I had to admit I did not know. What I felt, was that things were going to get worse but I wasn't going to elaborate.

I thought about the people left, Norman Broadbent the roadie, Chas French the guitarist who formed the group. Ray Guest the drummer, Allan Fender on keyboard and guitar and finally Rebecca Davis now Rebecca Rogan, my wife, and me, the protector and outsider, who would be next? To find out, I needed to talk to Rebecca and delve into her past something I knew would only make her illness and long term recovery worse. It was if her past life was behind a locked door, and the key didn't want to turn in the lock and reveal, what? Something dreadful had happened to Rebecca a long time ago, I was certain of it; I listened to the final song of the second and last album they had made.

'A Darker Shade of Blue'

Words by Rebecca Davies, Music by Stewart Walker/Ray Guest

I knew, I knew, I knew Our love

Was too good to be true

I knew the moment love dies
As I looked into your eyes
The colour of your lies

Was a darker shade of blue.
Woe, woe, woe,

Please don't leave me, I love you so

Don't let me go, Tell me that you

Love me,

Tell me, I need to know.

When I look into your Eyes, all I see are Worthless lies

The colour of the skies A darker shade of blue.
I hate you, I hate you,

I still love you, love you

Because, because, because,
Your eyes are full of lies the colour of the skies

your words of love are untrue,

but they're all I have

a darker shade of blue.

I googled the group 'A Paler Shade of Blue' and up popped several sites; I clicked on to one of them which had a group photo of them at the height of their limited fame. To the far left was Ray Guest, the drummer, with his long unwashed hair matted around an unshaven face that looked spiteful, he was wearing dirty battle fatigues and army boots he looked more like a punk than a jazz musician, then to his right, Rebecca the lead singer, wearing a skimpy white dress that hung of her thin shoulders, she looked ill, she wore nothing on her feet, but there was still a certain charm, a wistfulness about her In the centre was Chas French Lead guitar and backing vocals, smiling as always, clean cut and well dressed wearing a soft brown leather jacket pale blue silk shirt. He had the look of the main man, to his right was Stewart Walker, Saxophone, Guitar, Keyboards and Piano backing vocals, he was handsome but in a different way to Chas wearing a Levis shirt and jeans, cowboy boots and a broad smile and Allan Fender, Base and Keyboards on the end, he was wearing a heavy dark brown overcoat, a matching coloured fedora, and dark brown slacks, he looked cold and uninterested, as a group of successful musicians they didn't look like they were enjoying life very much, but that was not what was of interest to me. I looked closely at the photo; I knew what I was looking for. Ray Guest the drummer had grey dead pan eyes, Rebecca Amber, Chas piercing blue eyes, Stewart dark brown eyes and Allan eyes were brown as well, so it seemed to me Rebecca was singing about Chas, in the song 'A darker shade of blue'. I googled Chas French and it transpired that following the break up of the band 'A Paler Shade of Blue', he had formed two other groups 'Black Bird' and 'Fury' both with young women as the lead singers, neither band according to 'Rolling Stone' came to much, Chas gave up performing and ended up as a music producer with a record company, Blue Disc, based in Cornwall, he had married a Swedish girl Ingrid, almost a third of his age and had one child a girl they named Sissy aged three. It looked like Chas had done well for himself and like Ray Guest had joined the mainstream of society where music was a commodity, a way of relaxing rather than a way of life. My initial thought was that Chas was the missing link, the person; Rebecca was singing about on the album. I guessed Ray may have been jealous; he was after all the only one who had not been to bed with Rebecca. I know it's easy to get carried away and read into things which are not there but studying various photos of the band as a whole and then individually, I sensed that Chas was a bit of a narcissist, 'look at me, look at me', in some of the photos he looked spiteful, he wore an ugly sneer on his face when he should have been smiling, perhaps I was seeing what was not there but he didn't warm to me.

Rebecca would have been just seventeen when she joined the group and vulnerable to the attention of the main players,

Stewart, Allan and in particular Chas with his magnetic blue eyes, all much older than Rebecca. Ray Guest it seemed was the least successful with women and was the only one not to have bedded Rebecca, he rarely smiled in any of the group photos, he looked sallow and sullen as if he had lost a fiver and found a penny, always out of luck. Now though he seemed to be doing well, the house in Ham Common must be worth close to a million pounds, two cars on the drive best part of ninety five thou. A young wife, not the most attractive woman in the world but nice enough and two young children. Why now? After all these years did someone want to cause trouble? Everyone in the band seemed to be doing alright; the only one not enjoying the fruits of their modest success was Norman Broadbent the roadie. If I started to ask Rebecca about Chas, I was pretty sure she would see it as an inquisition and would seize up. Going to St Ives to speak to Chas would also be fraught with difficulties, foremost Rebecca would want to know where I was going and what was I getting up to. In the end I decided to wait for a suitable opening when I could bring the subject up. One thing was for sure, I needed to know much more about Chas French. The police came by the next day to undertake a forensic survey of 'the site' as they called it and to talk me over the questions they had put to me yesterday. I was in a truculent mood and had decided to stand my ground; okay I had shot Ivan in cold blood! But didn't see myself as a murderer, all I cared about was Rebecca's welfare. I was also mildly interested in where and when Ivan Reberoff had come from and how he was allowed to live in England how he had got hold of a gun excreta, excreta. When I asked Prendergast reluctantly confirmed from their enquiries that Ivan Reberoff was an unemployed Russian living in a rented flat in North Harrow, the landlord was a Norman Broadbent who lived in another part of the building, a breakers yard; that Ivan had no apparent income and no valid visa to allow him to be in this country. They were trying to trace the gun and the wad of six hundred pounds found in his wallet in crisp twenties. Prendergast looked embarrassed as he handed a file to his colleague and all I got was a blank stare. Then I asked them both if Ivan had a criminal record whilst living in England, trying not to laugh, whilst Prendergast wouldn't look at me, head down, coughing and spluttering in embarrassment, hand over his mouth reluctantly admitted that Ivan Reberoff had been charged and found guilty of GBH and burglary twice over a five year period and let off with a suspended sentence on his last attempt at villainy. I laughed out loud, saying it beggared belief that the immigration authorities and the police allowed Ivan Reberoff with no visible, income, a known criminal in England, two cases of GBH, and one case of violent robbery, with a string of criminal offences in Russia, was able to wander the streets of London, as if he was a regular law abiding citizen, gun in hand. They just continued to look at me, blank stares, shrugging their shoulders and saying nothing. I went on to say that it appeared to me, I was doing their job for them. Whatever case they had against me was unfolding before their eyes. Had they the police, the immigration authorities and the justice system of this country done there jobs properly, I would not have had to confront the monster Reberoff. I kept to my original answers and after an hour Peter Prendergast was seething, whilst his assistant Moira Anderson looked bored they had made no further progress, left the house with the same request. 'I was not to leave Esher without informing them'.

Chapter 9

28th February 2017

We are rarely forewarned of the worst things that can happen to us in life. If we knew what was before us we would take every measure possible to avoid disaster, occasionally we might get lucky but mostly it doesn't happen that way To say I wasn't prepared for the events that followed would be an understatement. It was a Friday afternoon, Bella was shopping and I had been messing around in my workshop with Pedro, we were wood turning, walnut tree goblets, my passion was equalled by his, as well as the wood turning we enjoyed each others company and Pedro was defiantly a guy who was better for knowing or so I thought. About half past four I went to check on Rebecca, she had been sleeping when I left her at two o'clock, I went into the room, she looked asleep and peaceful, then I noticed the envelope beside her right hand on the bed it was simply addressed 'David'

I looked at Rebecca again, she didn't seem to be breathing I touched her face gently and then her hand, she felt cold to the touch, I felt for a pulse, there was none. I ran to the phone and called for the ambulance which thank goodness arrived within five minutes. The paramedics two of them, a man called Frank and a young woman, Janice his assistant *(I never learnt their Surnames)* did all they could for twenty minutes but Frank the senior guy looked up and said,

"Sorry mate, she's gone, was she your wife?" I nodded to dumbfound to talk, Frank sent for the medical examiner, and of course the police. I could have hit Peter Prendergast the detective inspector investigating Ivan Rebroff's recent murder at our house; he had a smirk on his face as he strolled in.

"We're making a habit of finding dead bodies in your home Mr Rogan?" He quipped smugly, walking over to Rebecca's body which had not been moved and picking up the envelop by its edges and put it in a plastic zip bag in a gloved hand.

"Prendergast my wife has just died, I resent your flippant remark and request you give me the name of your superior, I am going to report you."

His face reddened as he fought to find what to say, he began apologising but I would have none of it. "It's too late for an apology and that letter you have picked up is addressed to me, I want the name of your superior." I glared at him.

"And if I choose not to give it to you?"

The smugness was returning to his face in a challenging smile.

"Then I will go through the usual channels, unless you are going to arrest me."

"There's no need for that Mr Rogan." A change of take, an apologetic tight lipped smile on his face.

"I profoundly apologise for my in appropriate words, now may we get on with the preliminaries of the police and medical investigation. We need to examine the envelop and its contents which is necessary and routine, we can do this immediately and I promise you no one will read the letter before you but you must realise this letter is evidence which most likely relates to her death and I may add, is not of our making, I will have the letter examined for finger prints, photographed, with luck I can have this back to you about eight o'clock to night, now if you will excuse me."

I still felt like I could hit him but calmed down, as I went down the stairs to get a much needed drink Bella came in her hands full of shopping, She knew immediately something dreadful had happened.

"What is it Senor David?"

Sit down Bella, she sat on the chesterfield and I told her I had just found Rebecca dead in her bedroom, most probably she had taken a massive over dose of some type of drug or drugs. The police and medical examiners are up there now." Without a word, Bella ran out of the reception room up the stairs and to her mistress's room, I could hear her crying and shouting Rebecca's name. It turned out when the police turned back the covers there was another letter this one addressed to Bella, Prendergast explained that for the moment she would also have to wait to read the contents, she nodded silently and left the room, no doubt to tell Pedro. By seven in the evening the street was awash with reporter's cars and television crews in addition to the police and ambulance vehicles. It was turning into a circus, this time I was going to do things properly and rang my solicitor Teddy Jacobs who lived in Bloomsbury.

He told me to remain calm and to do or say nothing to the police, without him being present. I was sure Prendergast would be pleased with this response.

"The police will try to badger you David but just say the only crime appears to have been my wife taking her own life and any questions which you will be happy to answer can wait until I am there with you."

I thanked Teddy and said I would 'take his advice'. I went to the drinks cabinet and poured myself a large whiskey and sat in the chesterfield, wondering what was in the letter. Bella and Pedro came in and we hugged and cried together for sometime before

Bella said she was going to make some tea. At half past eight Detective Inspector Prendergast came back and handed me my letter, he said nothing and at the time did not inform me that Bella had also received a letter, he still didn't trust me and suspected I was part of my wife's death, well I suppose it was his job to suspect people. I poured my self another large whiskey, the tea remained in the cup un-drunk and I read Rebecca's letter written in her neat hand writing.

My darling David,

Hopefully by the time you have found this letter I will be at peace and with my maker. I dare not think what effect this selfish act will have on you my darling and I know you will want and deserve explanation. Whatever I write I believe will be inadequate, but I owe you this.

I ran away from home when I was fifteen, I lived in Moss Side a suburb of Manchester with my parents, just the three of us I began to realise over a period of time that my father had an insatiable hunger for young girls and although I was his daughter, I was also a young girl coming to the age that was to his taste. I learned later, from Lilly Grant, my best friend who also lived on the Estate, that it was common knowledge to everyone other than my mother and me about my father's behaviour, but my mother wouldn't have a word said against him. From the age of fifteen, I worked in a shoe shop on Saturdays and saved some money, with the help of another friend, Kathy Brooks, whose family used to live three doors down from us, had moved to Newquay in Devon, Kathy phoned through her new address and I managed to get away before my father could take full advantage of me and lived with Kathy and her parents briefly before making some new friends in St Ives who were into music.

I had always wanted to be a singer. I was just over sixteen when I met Chas French and the rest of the band; they had come to one of my gigs in Newquay. Their lead singer, George Bradshaw a man from Sunderland, didn't cut the mustard so there was a spot for a singer. Me can you believe it!

I expect you can guess what happened next, yes I fell madly in love with Chas French, and his mesmeric blue eyes followed me everywhere. I was flattered, having the attention of an older man, everything was brilliant he told me he was going to make me into a star, of course I believed him, we played most nights and even if I say it myself, I was good and fitted in with the songs I wrote and the music they wanted to play. I was seventeen before I began to have suspicions that I wasn't the only woman in Chas's life, I learned through Stewart Walker, there was a wife living somewhere in Essex, and he had a daughter aged three, there were also a couple of groupies Patsy and Belinda and another girl called Margarita who had wanted to be their lead singer that hung around him. At first I was to full of it to notice, when I found out I blew a gasket. Chas was a serial womaniser was good at calming his women down and spinning them a line which they would stupidly believe and I was one of them.

To make matters worse like most musicians at the time, Chas dabbled in drugs, not the heavy stuff for him, just a little weed, but for some reason Chas decided that a daily injection of H would help me, in truth he needed me in the band, we were becoming popular and our first album 'A Paler Shade of Blue' was ready for release.

I expect you can guess the scenario of how I lived for the next four years; I am ashamed to say I became a junkie, full of H and booze. Chas was the one who obtained the only thing that was important to me H. For some reason my singing was even better, it had the edge that many great singers had, that lived for their next fix. Not that I am claiming in any way that I was in the same league as the greats, no way. To Chas's amusement I was passed around like a rag doll, first Allan, and then Stewart Walker, for some reason I never slept with Ray the drummer, there was something about him that made me cringe, of course he might have had me in my stupor, sometimes I slept for days if there wasn't a gig. I wrote most of the songs on our second album 'A darker shade of blue and I believe you had begun to put two and two together equalled Mr Blue Eyes himself, Chas French. One day he came in a filthy mood and if there is a discernable difference between making love or raping a junkie how ever small, I could tell the difference, but Chas couldn't or wasn't bothered, he raped me that night and then whenever he needed sex and Patsy, Belinda or Margarita weren't available. I wasn't completely brain dead and I knew that somehow I had to get away. I don' even remember if I received any money or wages; Chas looked after that side of things. I had a little money in a tin I kept under the bed, enough to get me away from St Ives, I had another friend Paula Green who had moved from Moss Side to Blackpool, she said she knew people who would help me in a Rehab centre where she worked if I could make my way to Blackpool. I managed to leave one Sunday morning after the band had crashed out after a gig and huge party afterwards and made my way to Blackpool by bus and train, it took me two days and I had to sleep rough but I was determined to get away and thank God I did.

I rang Paula when I arrived at Blackpool railway station, she met me and took me to the re-hab centre meet a doctor she worked for, I was lucky, I was admitted to St Anne's, where a group of dedicated nurses and doctors gave me my life back. Once I was better, I went to college to study accountancy and after twelve months got a job in Liverpool for a large company of accountants, I continued with my studies and was promoted several times before moving to PPP the London Accountants and Auditors.

My life was fine as long as I kept off the drugs and kept myself to myself, relationships with men of any kind were a no no, I trusted no one until you came along, the most beautiful and kindest man I have ever met and it grieves me, that I have taken the cowards way out, leaving you to mourn my darling.

It was the day Norman Broadbent phoned threatening me with blackmail that my past came surging back to me giant waves of fear washing over me and I need H as much if not more than I need you. I have resisted this urge for several weeks and Bella has been wonderful with me, she lost her sister to drugs and knew immediately what I was going through, I begged her not to tell you, I know you are kind but please do not ask Bella and Pedro to leave, for one thing you will need looking after and they love the house, but that is your decision now.

It would only have been a matter of time before I cracked and I could not have you spending the rest of your life looking after a junkie, there was also the publicity, which would have destroyed you and everything you had worked for, though I know you would gladly have accepted the undertaking. Bella has been so understanding to me and I thank her for that.

So I ask for you forgiveness and understanding. The sweetest of moments of my life have been with you and I thank you for that, when you sit in one of the courtyards in a sunny afternoon, think kindly of me

L

Rebecca

I put the letter down and made my way to my bedroom, I expected to cry again but I didn't, I just lay on the bed, initially numb. Had I known where to lay my hands on some H as she called it I would gladly have taken a bucket full, if it numbed the pain I felt and quelled the noise in my head but I was not as brave as Rebecca and choose to stay with my own poison, the brown liquid that came out of a bottle made and aged in Scotland. Before I was completely drunk I made my way to Bella and

Pedro's quarters and trying without being overdramatic told them that I would like them to stay for the foreseeable future but equally they were free to leave should they so wish. Bella opened her arms to me.

"There is much to be done Senor David, Pedro and me; we have to look after you now our mistress is gone."

I went back to my room and looked at my life through the rest of what was left in the bottle, listening to Rebecca's most poignant song of the second album 'A darker shade of blue' wishing it had been me that had gone to meet my maker and not her. Stewart Walker's sax blasted into the cold, silent night, the harshest and sweetest of rifts before he was joined by Rebecca's fragile voice, it was as if she was here, in the room, beside me, I felt a wave of warm air blow gently across my face as I listened to an apt song title, sipping my poison.

'The Day Jazz Died'

Words by Rebecca Davies, Music by Stewart Walker/Allen Fender

The day Jazz died I cried, and cried and cried

the pizzazz Razzmatazz Had un-wound

I listened to the sound Of broken notes

Falling to the ground Like a silent

Winters snow I died a little the day

Jazz died

The sky a brittle Cobalt blue

I realised something I always knew
There was a darker Shade, of blue

In the sky Watching waiting

For the music to die I cried the day

Jazz died

Chapter 10
1st of February 2017

When I woke in the morning and looked out of the front bedroom window, I could see a sea of reporters camped out on the pavement, I realised that I would need to say something if only to stop them printing whatever came into their heads, I thought about what to say, first of all the statement would be written and handed out in addition to my addressing the reporters verbally. I passed Prendergast in the hall he looked pensive. I stepped in front of him and he huffed in an exaggerated way I pointed my finger at him.

"If you so as much suggest that Rebecca did not write this letter Inspector or you hint that it has been written in my hand I shall thump you, very hard and to hell with the consequences."

"I must remind you," he said with the smirk visible, "that it is an offence to threaten a police officer Mr Rogan."

"You can remind whoever you like, Detective, I'm just reminding you that if you so dare as to make an insinuation I'll knock your teeth down your throat."

I walked off. I hated people like him who hid behind a badge, who were bullies and used their weapons when people were at their most vulnerable. I made my way towards the kitchen. He said nothing I had called his bluff, of course at the time I was still unaware that Rebecca had written to Bella as well, perhaps that's why he didn't go for me, he knew it was Rebecca's hand writing. He came running up to me. Mr Rogan, I came to tell you that Mrs Rodriguez has also received a letter from your wife, there is no question that anyone other than your wife wrote the letters, now if you will excuse me." I guessed why the hurry, in a few minutes I would have been in the kitchen and Bella would have mentioned her letter, it was all a game to the likes of Prendergast, what he really would have liked, was for me to have written the letters after having done away with my wife, the truth was he didn't like me, that was fair enough, I didn't like him either, but I wouldn't try to wrap a murder around him. I calmed down when Bella came out.

She had been handed her letter just before I bumped into Prendergast, neat timing.

She made some tea and we sat and talked, she showed me her letter asking if I wanted to read it, I said no, it was personal between her and Rebecca but I could imagine what was inside the letter.

Later I saw Prendergast get in his car, I went up to him and said, "I plan to take a few days holiday if you have no objection I am going to see Chas French, the man who allegedly raped Rebecca on numerous occasions and fed her H." He smarted from that one, I should have had the sense to shut up but I was angry.

"I want to find out for certain what happened, I reckon someone in the band wanted, Stewart Walker dead and then Rebecca, I believe Stewart was about to spill the beans and Ray Guest or Chas French employed Norman Broadbent to do their dirty work."

"Leave the detecting to us Mr Rogan," Prendergast said, the smirk was still there, I honestly believed he was enjoying himself.

"Are you going to arrest Chas French Detective for stealing her money, peddling dope and raping her on numerous occasions?"

"We need hard evidence Mr Rogan."

"That's why I am going down to Cornwall Detective."

"It's a police matter Mr Rogan."

"No, its about finding the truth, who abused and raped my wife and fed her Heroin, that makes it my business, He huffed and puffed then shaking his head as if to say, you're a crackpot, and drove off. Perhaps I was, I went to the study and began to compose the statement for the press.

Ladies and Gentlemen, I gather you are here standing in my garden wanting some sort of statement from me regarding my wife Rebecca's sudden death. Firstly I do realise hat you have a job to do and don't want to go away empty handed So I am giving you this statement for your reader's interest. There won't be another statement just this one so please kindly leave once I have made the statement, I will not be answering questions. Rebecca was the loveliest and most interesting person I have ever met; we had been together for just over 14 months. We were married in October last year.

In that short time our love grew and we were very happy, events changed when my wife was threatened with blackmail by a car breaker in North Harrow who used to be a roadie for the band 'A Paler Shade of Blue' of which Rebecca was the lead singer some twenty years ago.

She told me about the blackmail and I was able to deal with this successfully by letting the blackmailer understand that if he proceeded with his threats it would be worse for him than for Rebecca, I think he understood.

The tragedy was that it bought back all the memories of hardship she faced as a very young woman abused by most members of the group most who did nothing to help her and were mostly twice her age. Which was made double worse with the fateful gas explosion that killed

Stewart Walker his wife and two children and I extend my sympathy to his family and friends for their loss. The result of these two incidents I believe tipped Rebecca over the edge and brought about her suicide. The coroner and the police are of course doing their job and will have more accurate information on the sequence of events, I have gone into this amount of detail so you have a reasonable picture and to stop you from requesting more information from me. I request you allow me the privacy I need to grieve over my loss.

David Rogan.

I went out to face the journalists camped on my front garden and was greeted by a barrage of questions. I held my hand up and asked to be heard. Things quietened down and I began to recite my written spiel afterwards Pedro handed out hard copies, I thanked the reporters and asked them politely to leave my property, some had spoken to neighbours, to get the low down and background information about Rebecca and me. I imagined that Ray Guest, Norman Broadbent and Chas French had all gone into hiding, I was determined to find Chas though, I felt a little better in myself and decided how I was going to spend the rest of the day.

Chapter 11
2nd of February 2017

I spoke to my solicitor Teddy Jacobs in the morning and told him I was going to St Ives in Cornwall to talk to Chas French. I could tell he didn't think it was a good idea and why didn't I leave matters that required investigation to the police. I replied.

"Because if they find Chas French guilty of either rape of Rebecca, stealing her money or drug pedalling or all three, he is likely to get five year's max and be out in two and a half for good behaviour, or even less."

"Don't become a vigilante David."

He said, "No."

I replied, "I am going to talk to him first."

"Then what happens?"

"Depends on what he says, Teddy."

"I am afraid you are on your own on this one David."

"I know, I just wanted to let you know where I was going, okay."

I rang off and spoke briefly to Bella, she told me to take care. I said I would be back for the post mortem and she had my mobile number, there was a look of concern on her face but somehow it didn't register as concern over my welfare, perhaps I was being ungenerous. I was glad I took the plane to Exeter, where I had hired a car and by seven thirty I was holed up in small pub with a room over. The first pint slid down in five minutes and

I felt good, I had bought a map of Cornwall from the newsagents opposite and studied St Ives and the surrounding area. Chas's flat if it was the correct address was in the town centre, maybe five minutes front where I was sitting in the Union Inn, an old fashioned Public House. Was this one of his watering holes? I wondered if he came in for a pint, bit early for him I thought, though we had never met it was just a hunch and low and behold in walked the man, a huge smile on his face, with two women linking arm's either side, a brace of birds, they would say in Scotland. My hunch was half right, it was one of his watering holes, but I was wrong about the time. One of the women was a sassy looking blond about twenty three and the other a brunette even younger about nineteen, there were both what you might call pretty and were well formed in their tight but revealing dresses, it would have been difficult to think of Chas with anyone who was not drop dead gorgeous around him, he was one of those lucky men, he had the 'hey man look at me man' look as he entered the pub, I know it sounds a bit like sour grapes, probably is, most of us other men, take what we can get, whilst the Chas's of this world just stand still and the birds flock round and strangely this type of person is often equally popular with men someone to look up too, to be like. Me I would rather be dead than live the life of Chas French, well not exactly dead but you know what I'm saying. Chas walked up to the bar and ordered, "A pint of the usual John and two glasses of white wine for these two lovely ladies and one for yourself." Handing the barman a crisp £20 note. His smile was practiced to a fault, the two women drawled. I watched in amusement as he held court. I had to give it to him he was sixty four but didn't act or look a day over forty, the sun tan, blue blazer, grey slacks with pin point creases, white shirt open at the neck, smart casual clothes, manicured finger nails do wonders for men that want to be noticed and Chas in particular knew it. I thought for a moment he was looking at me but he was looking through me to someone who was coming into the pub via the car park.

"Simon," he said in a sauvé voice, sounding a bit like David Niven. "Meet Sandra and Becky."

The name Becky made me jump, I hoped he didn't notice, but he was to engrossed with his guests to notice me. I turned the page of my news paper and read the latest football results, whilst listening intently. From what I gathered Simon had the pick of the two, they were on there way to a club in Newquay. The girls giggled whilst they waited for the taxi and for Simon to make up his mind, from the way Sandra was moving her hand from one side of his trousers to the other it seemed she was Simons date for the evening, gloating like he had just won the lottery Simon had a soppy boyish grin on his face whilst Chas was giving Becky some spiel about a yacht, as smooth as silk.

I watched them leave amid much giggling and laughter was I becoming a sour puss? Perhaps! I felt sorry for Becky the younger girl who was going to be Chas's date for the night; she was going to be entertained on her night out by a master craftsman when it came to seduction, one that was three times her age. He probably used the same techniques on Rebecca twenty four years ago, refined charm, honed to perfection, over the years. I was watching a master at work but the charm if I guessed right would only last the night; Becky would be discarded as soon as he had had his fill, handed on to Simon who left to his own devices couldn't catch a cold would never have the nous to chat up Becky on his own. I ordered another pint, completed the crossword then went to my room. I was tired and it wasn't long before I was asleep. I enjoyed a full English breakfast in the morning and decided I would give Chas an hour or so before calling in and listening to what he had to say. The recording company was on the High Street, first floor over a ladies hair dressing salon another source of, on tap females. I was shown to a seat in a small reception room by Wendy, a fat woman, and I read the telegraph whilst I waited. About twenty minutes later a slightly worn looking Chas greeted me and ushered me into his office which as expected had all the trappings of success. Framed Gold discs adorned the walls with photos of he various groups and stars he had played with or managed.

"Now Mr Rogan how can I help you?" He folded his hands together. I had rehearsed my opening spiel and was interested on how he would react. I was surprised he didn't connect the name so I mentioned that I was Rebecca's husband. I noticed him give a sigh of relief.

"Dreadful matter," he said shaking from side to side.

"But what brings you down here?"

The blue eyes were piercing into mine, it was quite disconcerting and I imagine he was well practiced' I mentioned record royalties, and he breathed another sigh of relief.

"Oh, I am sure we can come to an amicable agreement, most of the songs were written by me and Beck."

Now he was smiling. I bristled at the shortened name but he didn't notice, he was thinking about money. Stewart and Rebecca's death were going to regenerate a lot of interest in the band and new record sales which followed the death of young musicians providing a windfall for the remaining members of the band, in particular the co authors of the songs and music.

"You really think the public are going to buy into, 'A Paler Shade of Blue'?"

"Yes," I said. "Big time if the number of reporters outside my house is any indication, Rebecca is going to be front page news, you too."

"Well every little helps," he said. "Can I get you a drink, tea, coffee?"

"No its okay thanks, I've just had breakfast, no what I really came to talk to you about was your relationship with Rebecca." Chas paused as he was about to say something, then changing his mind said, "It was a long time ago David, will it really help any of us to churn up the past surely it's better to allow things to rest as they are, I can understand you want answers to your questions, but some questions may not have any answers, it was after all over twenty years ago." I matched his stare until he blinked.

"I'm not sure I'm with you David." He was not going to give anything away until he knew the nature of my questions. He gave me the sort of 'honest John, I'll help all I can gov' look, which I matched that with my 'I am sorry to have to bother you but' look. I paused for a moment.

"Rebecca left me a letter, written just before she died there's some pretty detailed accounts of her time with the band and things that happened to her."

Chas looked pensive.

"May I see the letter, David?" The charm offensive coming into play with a sorrowful smile.

"I would gladly show you the letter but I don't have it Mr French, it's in the hands of the police something to do with evidence."

I watched keenly as I let the words sink in.

"Well she was a bit of a mess before she left the band, I realise this is painful for you David but she blamed everyone else for her problems which were mainly self inflicted I am sorry to say." He gave me what I thought was a disingenuous smile.

"You see," I said, "she states that at first you were both madly in love with each other."

"Look David we were in the music industry, people say all sorts of things to each other in the heat of the moment, you must understand that."

"Believe me Chas, I do, but in your case, you were what forty three and Rebecca had just turned sixteen when you met in Falmouth."

"Well age is no barrier to love in the music industry David."

"Yes Chas but you were also married at the time and had a three year old child."

"My you have been busy David, digging up the dirt, it won't get you anywhere; it's called title tattle."

He threw me a disingenuous smile that was meant to convey sympathy. These were the moments I now enjoyed most, when I took the Glock out and pointed it at him. He sort of half jumped out of his chair, them composed himself.

"Now what's this all about are you going to shoot me because I bedded your wife, twenty years ago, come on, she was begging for it David, I'm only human, she was a beautiful young woman and very manipulative."

I released the safety catch on the gun.

"No I'm not fussed about that Chas, but Rebecca alleges that you fed her heroin, turned her into a junkie and also raped her on several occasions, on top of taking her share of the groups money and keeping it for yourself, it's in the letter which the police have."

I watched him swallow and gripping his hands together to remain calm. "This is just untrue David, I never hurt Beck, please put the gun away."

I put the gun back in my inside pocket.

"The trouble I have Chas is that one of you must be lying." I gave him my version of a disingenuous smile. "I accept it could be either of you, but I ask myself why would Rebecca say such things about you and then take her life if what she said was untrue some twenty years on. If I had to make a guess as to who was lying I would say you, you are a serial liar, even last night you were on the game, whilst the wife and kids were in bed."

"They were at the grandmothers actually." I realised it was impossible to insult this man, he simply didn't care. I watched as he held back the need to laugh, having one over the dimwit of a wife must or perhaps she was just an ordinary human being trusting her husband on his night out, I felt faintly sick as I refocused.

"You lied to Rebecca, a sixteen year old girl who had left home for fear of her father raping her; you were married at the time and had a three year old child. Don't make me angry Chas or I will shoot you here and now, I am not fussed about going to prison."

He gave me an odd pleading look. I told him to get up we were going for a ride. I pointed the gun at him as we made our way back through the reception and out onto the street. I told him to get in the car and drove the automatic one handed as I kept the gun pointed at him. We drove to Paradise Park in Hayle and pulled up in a quite spot, we got out and sat on a wooden bench facing each other. I said to Chas. "Look I don't want to have to shoot you but you have to accept I cant let you get away scot free, I also don't want to break up your family, your child would suffer. "What about my wife?" He said, interrupting.

"She should have known better than to trust a rogue like you. I think a confession is best, a written confession, and then Detective Inspector Prendergast can decided what to do with you, its better than being knee capped."

I handed some paper and a pen, which I had ready. "It's your choice Chas."

"This is blackmail David; I wouldn't have had you down as a blackmailer, you all high and mighty."

"Yes in a way I suppose it is blackmail, but in the grand scheme of things, not as bad as rape and drug dealing, wouldn't you say?"

He rubbed his chin as if accepting defeat. "What do you want me to say, David?"

"Tell the truth for once, we can get your secretary, Wendy, to witness your signature alongside mine, then it will be a legal document."

He hummed and hard, then put the pen down. "I'm sorry David, I can't do it David, I just can't, it'll ruin me."

"I agree, but you will be ruined anyway, it will come out, this way you have a chance. Just think how much worse it would be if the reporters got hold of the story."

He picked up the pen and began to write, thirty minutes later he handed me the A4 piece of paper. "Will that do?"

I read his sterile words, it was pretty clear to me Chas didn't do empathy, I should have shot him there and then but I was trying to be reasonable. We went back to the car and I drove us to his offices where he called his receptionist Wendy a fifteen stone heavy weight, battle axe of a woman in her fifties, one of the few women in life who was safe, she was not his type. He told Wendy he wanted her to witness his signature only she didn't need to read the document. Wendy Billingsgate wrote her name and address beside mine, signed and dated. With that I bid Chas a good day, he looked forlorn, I suggested that when Prendergast got round to interviewing him he might suggest that all the proceeds from the record sales could go to a police charity, something which might make him consider not prosecuting you.

I got in the car and made my way back to Exeter and then caught the plane back to London by the time I got home I was exhausted and Bella made me a Spanish omelette with chunky chips, After two large glasses of Whiskey in my study, I went to bed and slept like a baby, pleased with my days work.

Chapter 12
5th of February 2017

Chief Detective Inspector Peter Prendergast called by to update me on the inquest which was to be heard next Tuesday. He also said I was needed to attend an interview and write a formal statement.

"Fine," I said. "Could we do this here?"

"Yes," he replied with a genuine smile. "But I will need Moira to attend would later this morning be okay."

"Fine by me," I said, I could tell he was making an effort to be understanding. In my saner moments I realised that there was no point to falling out with everybody. I decided to wait for the interview before giving him Chas's signed statement. I had begun to keep a diary of sorts. Prendergast turned up at twelve forty five, asking if there was somewhere quite we could go to for the interview. We made our way to the study where with detective Moira Anderson they conducted the interview. It was all pretty routine and Prendergast said that he had to ask some questions and was not trying to be offensive i.e. Were we happily married? Had we argued the day of her death? He did not query my answers and I found this very reassuring. When he seemed satisfied I thanked him and handed him Chas French's confession.

"I won't ask how you obtained this," he said with a smile.

"Actually it was quite easy in the end, I explained to Chas that whatever happened, you would eventually catch up with him and it would all come out, because of Rebecca's letter. So in reality, there was little choice, this way he has the opportunity for leniency. I admit I wanted to hurt Chas and not let him get away un-punished for what he had done to Rebecca. I realise now it's a police matter but had he been silly and mucked me about, you would be arresting me for murder."

"We wouldn't want to do that would we?"

It sounded as if we were old friends.

"I'll speak to him in due course but it will be the CPS which will decide whether to prosecute him or not. Mr French sounds like a nasty piece of work but not guilty of the murder of Stewart Walker and his family."

"Yes," I nodded, "that leaves Ray Guest and Norman Broadbent."

"I'll follow it up."

We said our goodbyes and I watched him leave, what next? James Pearson rang in the afternoon, he was Rebecca's solicitor to advise that he had the original signed 'Will' and as expected I was the only beneficiary. Nice to know but I was in no mood to celebrate. The next task was to inform Rebecca's friends and any relations of her death and what was happening. The coroner seemed to think the inquest which was to be heard next Tuesday would be straight forward so a provisional date of Thursday week was booked for the funeral to be held at Saint George's Church in Esher. There was I estimated about forty to fifty friends and family who would come to the funeral and refreshments afterwards we decided, that is Bella decided that it would be nice to have the refreshments at the house it was certainly big enough and we would employ caterers for the function but there was also a small function room at the Bear

Hotel in the event that the numbers were so few, we put the final decision on ice I wasn't so sure about the numbers.

Chapter 13
February 9th 2017

There were three main issues:

1. I had killed Ivan Reberoff and at the very least would be charged with manslaughter perhaps murder, most likely a prison sentence.
2. What to do about Norman Broadbent in my book he should be eliminated permanently.
3. What to do about Ray Guest, he was I believe the one who employed Norman to blackmail Rebecca and somehow do away with Stewart Walker and his family. I needed to be sure, I didn't mind ending up in jail but not for eliminating an innocent man. I wondered who I had become since the abortive blackmail, my killing Ivan Reberoff, Stewart Walkers death and following Rebecca's death reading her letter.

I had turned into a mad man, a monster like Ivan but much, much worse. I had killed in cold blood, I had blackmailed, and I had kidnapped Norman Broadbent and could easily have shot Chas French but didn't, *something in my favour*, in my saner moments I tried to analyse myself to find out why I was thinking and behaving the way I was. I knew I needed to pull myself together and stop wanting to kill everyone. Rebecca would not have wanted that but I needed to find out who was behind the blackmail and if there was anything else to come out of the woodwork. I was pretty sure Norman was the blackmailer but on whose behalf. Chas unlikely, Allan Fender had moved to Australia ten years ago, even more unlikely, which left Ray Guest the only one who had not bedded Rebecca. The likeliest candidate maybe another visit was called for? But I had to be careful not to tread on Prendergast toes I was in my study when Bella came in looking anguished.

"What is it I asked."

"It's my mother she has broken her arm, she fell in the street, she can't do very much in her house and she has to care for my father who suffers from arthritis I may have to go home for a while. But I want to look after you as well I promised Rebecca." I thought for a moment.

"You could bring your parents here if you want there is plenty of room."

"I couldn't impose on you like that Senor David." She had the sweetest smile. "You wouldn't be imposing," I said, adding.

"It's what you feel is best. If you want them here I can pay for the flights?"

"I'll speak to mother and see what she says thank you Senor David." It was so strange I had known Bella and Pedro Rodriguez for just over two months and it was like I had known them all my life, I had never met anyone who was as attentive and dedicated for Rebecca's wellbeing as Bella had been. She was first class in my book; if she wanted her mother over it was fine with me, it was the least I could do. An hour later she came in and said Angelo her mother's neighbour would drive them to Malaga airport see them on to the plane tomorrow morning if we could collect them from Heathrow.

"No problem," I said. "Your parents can have any of the bedrooms they are all en-suite." She came over and gave me a big hug.

"Thank you so Senor David, it means so much, I will be able to attend my mistress funeral."

The next morning we were all stood in the arrivals concourse waiting for the flight from Malaga to Heathrow to land it was on time and I watched as Bella's mother walking her arm in a sling and her husband in a wheelchair pass through baggage reclaim customs and join us. There were tears and kisses hand shakes and hugs, before we made our way to the airport taxi I had hired. By two o'clock we were back in Esher and an hour later Bella's mum and dad and Pedro were sat in the courtyard enjoying a cup of tea. I didn't really feel like celebrating, but the love and joy between them as a family was infectious, so I agreed when asked, to join them for dinner I wondered how her mother would manage. I needn't have worried Bella made paella and her mother managed adequately with a fork it had been a while since we dined in the dining room, it was very pleasant and dignified but there was an elephant or perhaps a ghost in the room 'Rebecca' none the less Bella and her parents enjoyed themselves and I retired early leaving them to it. It was nice to hear other voices in the house it was too bright and airy to be a place of sadness.

Chapter 14

February 13th 2017

I was on my way out to work. I'm not sure what made me go into the study and pick up the land line phone. Tt was eight o'clock, a Friday morning and I was running late, I realised the phone was in use. It was Bella; she was talking to a man. I never liked the idea of listening into other peoples phone calls, if I really was a gentleman I would have put the phone down. Why I didn't I can't say.

"It's ok, Norman," Bella said.

"Senor David has left for work, so it's safe to talk."

"I've ad Ray Guest on the blower bell, wants to know when we are going to complete, ees got old bill brevin dan is neck."

"Well, Ray will just have to wait Norman, I'm not a magician."

"Give me somefin to tell him, Bell."

"Tell him David's new will has been prepared, I am hoping to get Senor David to sign it on Thursday, then it's up to you, the quicker the better."

"Fanks Bell."

I heard a click and the line go dead. I began to sway for a moment and had to sit down; I couldn't believe what I had just heard. It seemed there was a conspiracy to kill me once I had signed the new will leaving my estate to 'The Margarita Rodriguez and Rebecca Rogan Foundation'. I didn't know the extent of the subterfuge but it seemed to me I had been taken as a complete fool. I needed to get out of the house before Bella found out that I had not left for work. As bad luck would have it as I came out of my study, Bella walked into the reception room. She looked at me a frown on her face, I had never seen before.

"I thought you had left for work Senor David?" I smiled and found my footing. "I had Bella but I forgot something, silly me, had to come back for my notes."

I shook my head like an absent minded professor. She didn't answer immediately, I could tell she was thinking, then she said. "Have you found your notes, David?"

"Yes, thank goodness, beside my diary." I smiled again;

"Look I really must go Bella; I was late before I had to turn back." She gave me another doubtful stare as I made my way to the hall. "See you later," I added trying to sound up beat.

"Okay Senor David, have a nice day."

That was better, I hurried out to the car and drove off, my mind swirling with confusion and disbelief, no matter what I had over heard on the phone' I could not bring myself to believe Bella was scheming to get me to sign a new will leaving my estate to the foundation, which was to be run by her.

The problem was she had been talking to Norman Broadbent and he was an A1 criminal. I needed to think, but my mind was all over the place.

I left the car at Esher Station and got the train into London Waterloo, I arrived at the Brooke Street offices at twenty to ten, I didn't like being late and neither did Charlie, he looked up as I past his office.

"Are you alright David? You look rather done in, if you don't mind my saying so, don't feel obliged to come in if you are unwell."

I gave him a hand wave and a friendly smile of reassurance.

"I'm fine thank you Charles." I went to my office and began looking at my notes, there was a meeting at ten and I was to attend.

Charlotte, the new PA shared by three of us bought me in a cup of coffee. "Thank you Charlotte, just what I need."

I watched her walk back to her own small office, the way she walked made a mans heart beat faster and she knew it, though not appropriate I realised I was getting my mind back into functioning mode. The meeting went well, I wrote up some more notes and happily for me my work was done, I could stay or leave the office, there were no rules, they liked what I did for them during my two days a week and trusted me implicitly. I thought I knew the meaning of those words as Charlotte came over with a draft of my notes. I had trusted Bella implicitly and now I had found out she was a fraud, to what extent I did not know, I needed to think it through before I returned to my home, 'the lions den' if I wasn't careful I was going to end up as dead meat. In some ways it didn't matter, I was past caring about myself, after losing Rebecca I believed I had little to live for, hence my being so gung-ho. I always thought there was something wrong with Bella but could not put my finger on it, I realise now what was wrong. Everything had been too perfect. Now I had a moving plot to solve and my fore-finger which was trying like mad to pin point the sequence of the plot was shaking like mad, "get a grip man" I said to myself "or you'll end up like Rebecca and Stewart, dead".

At twelve I rang home, Bella answered, I wanted her to notice by reading the number on the phone that I was calling from work."

"Hello Bella."

"Senor David." She spoke cautiously, not like her; I made sure I spoke evenly not to cause alarm.

"Something has come up, I am going to be in Brighton for the rest of the day and probably tonight as well."

There was a prolonged pause; I could sense her thinking before answering. "Is everything alright Senor David?"

"Yes I'm fine; it's an old friend in a bit of trouble, asked if I could help."

"Will you be back before Friday; there's the will to sign."

"Of course," I said blithely, I was not very good at lying, I needed more practice.

She closed the call, sign the 'Will', sign my death warrant more likely, I needed time and space to think. Then I had a brain wave, I rang Winston.

"Winston?"

"Yes, don't tell me it's David Rogan, how are you my man?"

"I'm fine Winston; tell me if I remember right, your wife is Spanish?"

"Yes she is my man, Isabella or Izzy as I call her is the most beautiful Spanish woman in England." I could imagine him smiling.

"I'm after a favour, a paying favour Winston; your wife might be able to help me."

"We all like favours that pay my man, how can we help you?"

"Do you think Isabella could see what she can find out about a young Spanish woman of the name, Margarita Rodriguez, she would have been between seventeen and twenty years old, I believe she lived in Madrid before coming to Newquay and then St Ives, she was a singer and knew the band 'A Paler Shade of Blue' she died about twenty years ago, her body I think would have been returned to Spain." I paused then added, "Rebecca mentioned Margarita in the letter she left me, her parents and sister Bella two years older also lived somewhere in Madrid."

"Cool Man, I have two of the Shades records, Izzy likes Jazz. Shouldn't be too difficult if there is anything to be found, Izzy loves the net, she will look there first and then face book, ring some of her friends if necessary, is this urgent, my man?"

"Sort of Winston."

What is the paying part of the favour may I ask my man?"

I hadn't given it a thought. Well what about thirty pounds an hour, minimum three hundred pounds for your trouble and five hundred if you come up trumps."

"What if we come up with nothing, my man?"

"Just bill me, three hundred for your trouble, money isn't the issue here, I need some background info on Margarita, Winston."

Leave it with me my man, I'll come back some time to night or tomorrow with an initial response my man."

"Thanks Winston." I put the phone down and felt better for it. I headed off back to Esher on the train and then drove to Brighton where I booked into a rather nice, sea front hotel. I had always liked Brighton and had happy memories of holidays there with my parents, the last two weeks in August, every year until I was twelve, without fail. I had a bucket full of coloured pebbles which I kept in my bedroom until my parents died and I sold the house. I wonder sometimes if the new owners kept them. I booked into a sea front hotel in Hove. When I went up to my room the first thing I did was open the lap top and I started to list my assets Actually I had no idea what I was worth since Rebecca's death, I had been too busy. God when you think of it, Rebecca hadn't been dead more than two weeks and they were plotting my demise, were these people that desperate or were they just greedy and evil, I was inclined to believe the latter. I tried to calm down and helped myself to a miniature bottle of Whiskey from the mini bar. I fired up the laptop and opened a new word document file and began typing.

Description	**Min.**	**Max.**
House in Esher	£1.5m	£2.5m
Money in current account	£12, 000	£12000
Money in savings account	£750.000	£750,000
Premium bonds	£100,000	£100,000
Rebecca's jewellery	£225,000	£500,000
Cars	£50,000	£80,000
Paintings in house	£40,000	£60.000
Stocks and shares	£600,000	£700,000
Offices over shop in Edgware	£650,000	£750,000
Miscellaneous	£10,000	£15,000
Total	**£3,912,025**	**£5,522,045**
Plus		
Royalties from record sales	*£250,000*	*£1,000,000*

A lot of money but split three ways, I checked the split out, thinking Norman would get around one hundred thousand plus for doing the dirty work and disposing of me, 10K for each of the heavies. I figured the rest would be split fifty fifty between Bella and Ray Guest, two to three million each, a tidy sum but a chilling thought. I then listed out the sequence of events from the first aborted blackmail to the murder or unfortunate gas explosion which killed Stewart Walker and his family and then Rebecca's death.

One thing had always struck me as odd, Bella didn't look anything like or have any of her mother or fathers mannerisms, was I imagining it, or was I loosing my confidence and ability to reason? One thing I would do was get some samples of Bella and her parent's hair and have her DNA checked if the opportunity arose.

If they were Bella's parents, where did they fit in? Probably another set of eyes and ears to check on what I was doing in the house, if she was out, and Pedro was the beef, if it was needed, he was much younger and stronger than me but not as demented, which perhaps was in my favour. There were three lines of attack, Ray Guest in Ham Common, Norman Broadbent in North Harrow and Bella and Pedro Rodriguez and her parents living in my house in Esher. I had to remove one of them as quickly as possible to reduce the odds, the most obvious was Norman Broadbent, 'the hit man' but I thought he would have brought in some stronger protection than the hapless Ivan, so if I was going to tackle him a recognisance mission was needed. When I got back home, I parked up and took a taxi to Richmond to see an old friend of mine in the motor industry.

I explained to Rod Grove my friend and the owner of the showroom that I needed an old car or van preferably which I could use for surveillance purposes. Rod gave me a funny look but for some reason didn't ask questions and agreed to my request and took me round the back of his showroom and showed me a battered old ford van, it might have been white or light grey once, it was perfect for my purpose. "It's seen better days David but you can have it for a couple of days for two hundred pounds and a deposit of five hundred in case you don't manage to bring it back."

He gave me a knowing smile. I had done Rod a few favours over the years, planning drawings for an extension to his house in Twickenham, and the same for an extension to the rear of the car showroom, without charge, in this respect, I thought two hundred was a bit steep but I wasn't in a bargaining position, I needed a van and this one was perfect. Rod said he used it for taking car parts to the scrap dealer in East Sheen, where itself would be going shortly, the main thing was it was taxed and insured and though a little noisy to say the least, drove well, starting up first time and he didn't need it back, probably end up as reported stolen by Rod, at the moment that was the last thing on my mind, I had a motor which was perfect for my use.

Rod and I went back to school days, we lived in the same street and went to the same school, at one time we were best of friends but had over the years drifted apart, we had different social circles, well Rod did, I didn't have any since Jane's death and even less after Rebecca's. Primarily Rod was a business man, sales were slow and he needed the money, I thanked him and handed him over two hundred in readies and a cheque for five hundred and then I was on my way to North Harrow to check out the opposition. I could see Rod standing on the forecourt scratching his head, as he watched me pull away, probably wondering what I had got myself into, bottom line, he didn't want to know, business was business he had his sale, but the motor trade was notorious for keeping stum. I stopped at a camera shop and purchased a video camera, monitor and an old SLR Practica with a zoom lens and some film. I stopped at a local supermarket and stocked up on biscuits tonic water and some chocolate I had already packed the gun in my brief case and a set of clean clothes. I drove around the crescent twice Norman's breakers yard was on the junction with the main road, before deciding where to park up. I found a space about thirty yards away on the opposite side of the main road; the pub was a further eighty yards down the road behind ne. I would like to have been closer but I didn't want to be too obvious. I made myself as comfortable as I could and began the wait it was four o'clock I felt I was in for a long wait but at half past five, I saw Norman park-up an old Beige Merc on the forecourt. Two big men got out of the car and stood looking around, the biggest and ugliest by far was about forty five, six four, eighteen stone and legs as thick as tree trunks, he had a round ruddy face with a flattened nose, he was bald on top with a gold loop in his left ear, and wore a shiny black suit over a dark grey shirt and pumps, probably an ex bouncer. His mate a shade younger and two inches shorter came in at about fifteen stone, he looked more regular with a dark grey sweat shirt jeans and brown shoes, his face was more angular and he had his blond hair cut short into a Buzz cut, his stocky arms and neck were covered with Tattoos, I had him down as ex army type, much more dangerous than his ugly colleague, who I noted was in charge. After a minute or so Norman emerged from the car smoking as usual wearing his long black leather coat, black brimmed hat, and black boots, they walked three abreast to the flat over at the rear of the yard. I snapped all three as well as the videos recording which I had set up by making a hole in the side facing the forecourt, it wasn't ideal but would do. After they went in, I awaited five minutes then got out of the van the road was clear not a soul in sight, so I quickly slashed three of the car tyres with a Stanley knife and nipped back to the van. I was lucky two minutes later the beef cake came out and opened the boot, and took something out in a brown holdall, then closing the boot lid with a bang, made his way back to the flat. I was amazed, beef cake hadn't noticed the slashed tyres, it was like watching a carry on film. I noticed a space across the road about thirty yards further back, it was less conspicuous so I drove around the block and parked up, and helped myself to a cheese sandwich. I suppose I might have missed them but they couldn't have gone far with three flat tyres. At eight o'clock I heard a noise, it was Mr Tattoo closing the front door, they walked three abreast wearing the same clothes, to the car and using the same surveillance technique, the beef looking around, satisfied they got in the car, Norman first, lighting up a small cigar in the back, then Beef cake wearing a homburg which made him look like Munster of the Adams family and then Mr Tattoo who got in the driver's seat. I watched as he turned the ignition key release the hand break and drove off, they drove about four yards and stopped. Mr Tattoo got out and walked around the car, Norman had wound the window down and all three seemed to be talking then Beef cake followed by Norman got out and the three of them commenced walking around the car. Norman lighting up another cigarette, removing his hat, pointed to something. Mr Tattoo got down on his knees and began to measure the size of the slash to the passengers back tyre; they continued to walk around the car Norman scratching his head as if in a daze. Eventually they went back to the flat.

Norman was sitting in his favourite arm chair, with a gin and tonic and customary cigarette to hand trying to work out who had it in for him, after careful thought, there were in his opinion only three possibilities. The Tottie brothers, Italy's version of the Kray Twins, Albescu, Neguescu and the younger Lacusta Bolohan, the notorious Romanian brothers who controlled much of north London, Wembley being their last acquisition, Harrow was next on their list and finally there was the idiot Architect David Rogan, he found it hard to believe it could be me, he believed it took a certain in built hardness that only experienced criminals had, to take on the likes of himself, if it was Rogan he was way out of his depth but to be safe and Norman was a careful man, he ran the possibilities over again. Okay Rogan had got lucky with the abortive black mail attempt last June, that was seven months ago and there was nothing to link Norman to what Bella and Ray had in mind for him next. Only three people knew, himself, Bella and the poof Ray Guest who was up to his head in debt, unless Bella or Guest had tipped off David Rogan he couldn't have known. Consuming the last of his drink, Norman was clear in his mind, David Rogan hadn't slashed the tyres of his car, which only left Tottie and Bolohan brothers, he tended to think the worst, the Bolohan brothers were using him, *'a small fish'* as a warning to other *bigger fish* that they meant business. He would ring Marco Tottie in the morning and have a man to man, if he was right he would swing in with the Totties until the Rogan business was complete and he had got his pay off, one hundred and fifty large, then all being well he would move to Spain or Tenerife. It was getting to be too much like hard work in North Harrow; he lit another cigarette, poured a generous amount of gin into his glass, no tonic this time and decided to be on the safe side, he needed to recruit more muscle. Twenty minutes later a taxi pulled up an all three came back out and they got in the taxi. I watched them drive off towards Wembley, boys night out, I figured. I contemplated what to do next, wait till they came back or mess up the flat a little. I decided making a mess might be good. Luckily there was still nobody about or I didn't see anyone, I could easily have been seen from a window but this road didn't have the nosey parker feel, people kept themselves to themselves in this neck of the woods. The wrecking brace forced the front door open; I didn't expect an alarm to go off after all the muscle was Norman's deterrent; I quickly made my way up the stairs.

The flat was surprisingly neat and had some nice furniture, I noticed a print of Monet's water lilies over the gas fire in a large frame, Norman had taste after all.

I put the plug in the kitchen sink and switched on the hot and cold water taps, did the same in the bathroom with the wash hand basin, then trashed the wardrobes in the two bedrooms, I noticed a bundle of ten and twenty pound notes on Normans bed side cabinet, I pocketed those and then left the freezer door open and pushed the sideboard over in the living room, I could hear the sound of breaking glass and china. When I left, the flat was a mess as intended, the water from the sink and bathroom was just beginning to pool on to the floor in the hall. Surprisingly the front door locked after me, which was good. I made my way across the yard and returned to the van and had a second cheese sandwich and some tonic water. I figured it would be about twelve o'clock when they would get back; I was fifteen minutes out, a taxi pulled up at eleven forty five. They looked tired and worse for wear as Norman back to smoking cigarettes paid off the taxi driver. They were greeted with a wave of water as they opened the front door which they couldn't push open fully until the water had subsided. I burst out laughing when. Beef cake came crashing back down the stairs; I presume losing his footing on the wet stair treads and did a back summersault on to the forecourt his legs in the air. It was time to move, as I started the van Mr Tattoo came running out towards me, holding a gun. And shouting. "Hey you!"

I put the van in gear and floored the gas pedal the old van sprang into action and I headed straight for him. I caught him a mighty side swipe to his left side throwing him and his gun into the air, I saw him in the mirror trying to get up but he fell back down, something for Norman to ponder I said to myself, feeling the adrenalin rush. I made to turn left to get out of North Harrow as quickly as possible but at the last minute I turned right instead, which would bring me back to them, but from the opposite direction. I nosed quietly, well as quietly as the old van would allow given it had been round the clock twice, into the street, Norman was standing behind Mr Tattoo who was still on the ground, with Beef cake trying to pull him up, I floored the gas again and the old beauty shot forward, there was nowhere for them to go. I could see the horror on their faces, rather than run them over, two messy; I took another side swipe as I turned the steering wheel away from them to the left at the last moment, hitting all three of them. When I looked in the mirror the three of them were rolling around on the floor, someone from the pub had come out and I guess was calling an ambulance. It was no time for faint hearts, I told myself, it was them or me, the beauty of attacking criminals was that they were unlikely to give the police the full story, so my guess was that Norman would give some cock and bull story about turf wars and Ray and Bella would make sure the muscle kept their mouths shut but it would be at a cost, I know it sounds dreadful but I was rather pleased with myself. The muscle had been eliminated and I was now dealing with two enemies not three. I didn't drive the van back home or to Rods showroom, but drove to Edgware where I had a lock up I inherited from my father business. It was located in a row of garages behind my father's old plumbing shop which had a flat over which I had used as an office. I drove the van into the empty garage locked up and hired a taxi back to Richmond where I picked up my old Mondeo and drove home. Bella was waiting anxiously and asked if I was alright. I had told myself the only way to beat these people was to act normal, however much I would like to do something else, I needed to know if Bella was involved in Rebecca's death. I smiled and thanked her profusely and asked after her mother and father. She said. "Yes, they are fine and I have made a Spanish dish, would I like to join them for supper."

I said, "Yes I would love to, your so thoughtful Bella." I was playing her game, if that was what was required. Smiling at my compliment she said my solicitor had phoned and the 'Will' was ready to sign.

"Great," I said, adding, "I'll go first thing great idea of yours the last thing we would want is the government getting their hands on my money." Anyway I said, "I hoped to be around for a little longer." I paid special attention to Bella's face as I spoke, not a trace, nothing that suggested 'we'll see about that', as she came over and caressed my arm.

"Nothing can happen to you Senor David, Pedro and I are here for you." She smiled again saying, "I'll see you at eight for dinner."

There was no doubt about it Bella was a flawless actress I could almost believed her! I was safe in her and Pedro's hands. When I got to my room. I counted the money I had taken from Norman's bedroom. Eighteen hundred pounds dead up, a tidy sum for Norman, I wondered whether they had made the news and switched on the television. There was a slot on the local calendar news, which reported that three men had been seriously injured in a hit and run incident in North Harrow, the police were calling for witnesses to contact them. There were no other details. I switched off the television and thought about what to do next. My mind was a blank and whatever I needed to do would have to wait until the morning, suddenly I felt very tired and slept till seven, when I took a shower and dressed for dinner in casual clothes.

The dinner was as always enjoyable Bella's parents seemed to be settling in. No one spoke though through out the meal, was that a sign of a guilty conscience, I admit I felt guilty. I would give anything to know if they were her real parents or part of the subterfuge for now I could only surmise. I left them to it and retired early.

Chapter 15

14th February 2016

The next morning I set off for Teddy's offices after my breakfast drove slowly and had the feeling I was being followed so I slowed down to make sure I didn't lose my tail it looked like a woman driving. I pulled up outside Teddy's office and watched a blue polo pass by it was a woman and I was pretty sure it was Bella but it was only a fleeting glimpse, if it was her, where did she get the car and where did she keep it? She had some nerve if it was her but I knew that already. After the normal, hellos and how are you keeping, Teddy gave me the 'Will' to sign, I was delighted to see four typing errors and he had missed my middle name 'Peter' out. Teddy apologised profusely saying Mary his secretary wouldn't be in until Monday and could it wait until then?

"Of course," I said, putting my copy with the spelling mistakes in my briefcase. Bella would not be happy though, I didn't know why and I was sure she would want sight of it. Whatever was meant to happen had I signed the 'Will' would now have to wait; it bought me two more days, and time, for a trip to Ham Common to see Ray Guest again. When I returned home, I was greeted by Bella as I expected.

I pretended to be furious with my solicitor and threw the copy of my 'Will' down on my desk.

Bella said, "May I?"

In any other circumstances I would have considered her impertinent but she needed to see it, so I nodded acting dumb as she readily picked it up and read it.

"Why couldn't they make the changes today, Senor David?"

"Because my Solicitor's damn secretary only works for him three days a week, it will be Monday afternoon can you believe it?" I put on a show of being very angry but I sensed she was much angrier than me, of course she didn't know but I was delighted it had bought me two more days and cost Bella, two days, for what reason I had no idea.

"Well at least I can count on you Bella I don't know what I would do without you, you are a rock." I gave her my warmest smile.

"Thank you Senor David, as always, the pleasure is all mine." Her eyes were telling me something or was I losing it completely.

"I think I might go back to Brighton this weekend my friend still needs my help.

I could see my latest travel news was irritating her, probably because she would lose control of knowing where I was and what I was up to.

"Forgive me for asking but is it a man you are helping?"

In any normal event I would have considered this question also impertinent but we had passed the normal protocol sometime ago.

"Yes Bella, my friend Malcolm an old school chum, has cancer its terminal." I had mentioned the name Malcolm before; she hadn't been listening, unusual for Bella. I could feel the breath of relief pass between us and her line of thought, thank goodness it wasn't a woman, she was hard at work trying to second guess me and a little jealous of an imaginary woman. This confirmed what I had begun to think about Bella, she wanted me, and if she couldn't have me because we were on different sides, no one else would get the chance. I thought how ridiculous we all are with our emotions and tangled loyalties. She came over and touched my arm like she had earlier. It was a come on, one of us is going to die but that does not mean we can't share some special moments together. It was a coded message and I got it. She let her hand rest on my arm for a few moments; I could feel her fingers kneading my skin. I moved away reluctantly, ashamed that she had caused me to feel desire. What was happening to me? We hadn't even buried Rebecca. I felt sick, suddenly I needed some fresh air and to get away from the house and Bella.

Chapter 15
15th February 2017

I packed a few items of clothes for show and a tooth brush and told Bella I would be back no later than Monday morning when I would go over to my solicitor and get the 'Will' signed. I checked carefully in my mirror to see if I was being followed but was pretty sure I wasn't. Perhaps Bella had better things to do? I enjoyed the short drive to Ham Common; and listened to the second album 'A darker shade of blue' There was a song I had heard briefly but not properly listened too, 'Green Eyes,' the last track on side two, it was written by Rebecca she would have been about nineteen or twenty at the time.

'Green Eyes'
Words by Rebecca Davies, Music Stewart Walker

You had the keenest

Greenest green eyes I've ever seen Sharp and bright

Bitter and mean That filled the skies With jealousy

And your lies When first we met In St Ives.

We loved the same man Sang the same songs

I never noticed your thorns and prongs

The jealousy in your green eyes So big it filled the skies

With your lies Hatred and cries

That rumbled like thunder In the skies

A blazing sheen of Auroras green

So sad I had to find out Your jealousy and Bitter lies were about
The man I had

How sad,

But now you are gone I share your grief
There is no comfort Or relief
in Jealousy and desperate lies

Good bye green eyes
Take with you

A darker shade of blue

It would be interesting to know who Green Eyes was, whoever she was, she had little time for Rebecca, part of the twenty year old puzzle, another one of Chas's women no doubt, but I thought something more. I arrived at Ham Common at eleven o'clock and made my way to the leafy lane where Ray lived. There were two cars in the drive so I guessed Ray was in. I had thought on the journey what I would say if he caught me unawares, the best tack was the one I had initially used with Chas, talk about the royalties from the re-release of the two albums 'A Paler Shade of Blue' and 'A darker shade of blue' which were numbers one and two in the play lists, since Stewart and then Rebecca's deaths. The recording industry does not have time to mourn when there is good money to be made. I got out of the car and walked up the drive to the front door, it opened as I was about to ring the door bell.

"What is it this time?" Ray Guest asked standing in shorts, a black Sabbath top and sandals a New York Yankee's cap and a scowl on his face.

"Yes I am sorry to turn up unannounced Mr Guest but I want to discuss the royalties for the albums if you have a few moments."

"Couldn't we have done this over the phone Mr Rogan?"

"Yes of course we could, I just thought, well you might be pleased at the news and we could discuss the matter, I know it's a sad time but I also think its great time getting full recognition for your music."

"Yeah, Yeah Yeah, you had better come in then, the wife's just taking the kids shopping and then to the cinema."

I could see him visibly relax but the look of suspicion never quite left his face. A few minutes later his wife and the two the children came in through the open lounge.

"See you later Ray," his wife said as they walked to the front door. She turned to look at me, and then Ray, but he didn't introduce me to her, it suited me as much as I guessed it suited him. I was glad to remain anonymous. Alone Ray opened the conversation.

"What did you have in mind then Mr Rogan?" I didn't have the luxury of time either. At any moment he might decide to text or ring Bella on his mobile or she might just ring him, so having wormed my way into his house, I put plan 'A' into action straight away, pulling out the Glock. He looked startled and then tried to smile. "What's this about?"

I looked at him and said.

"I happened to overhear a telephone conversation two days ago, Bella my house keeper was talking to Norman Broadbent."

His face visibly shrunk, the game was up whatever was going to happen next, he knew it was going to involve pain, he had been found out.

"Yes, Norman Broadbent was quite concerned about my signing my 'Will' before Friday, he had been talking to you apparently and you said there was no time to waste, you were the next port of call for the old bill."

I stopped and watched to see his reaction.

"This wasn't about you my friend, yes I admit I had been speaking to Norman but it was about Chas French, he's the one you should be chasing, and he's the blackmailer and womaniser. Another piece of the jigsaw fell into place, how would Ray have known about Chas, now I was sure Ray was the third party in the plot to murder me.

The next task was to make sure that Bella didn't get to know that Ray was out of the game. I had planned to take Ray to the flat in Edgware, whilst I tackled Bella and Pedro and whoever mum and dad were, that on its own was a task four against one even if mum had a broken arm, she could still fire a gun if she had too, I wasn't going to leave anything to chance, my nerves had become jangled, I needed to calm down.

My best and strongest strategy was always going to be surprise, so it was vital Bella thought Ray was okay. I might have to risk a phone call, I told Ray to phone his wife saying he had some business in Birmingham and would be back Monday morning. He didn't like it one bit, but the gun persuaded him this was the best course of action.

That went smoothly now a similar call to Bella much more risky. As luck would have it she did not answer so he left a message adding that the place he was staying was a farm and not to worry if she could not get hold of him as there was no internet coverage. I handed Ray the hand cuffs told him to put them on and we set off for Edgware. The journey was uneventful and we arrived back in London around three thirty we parked around the back in front of my garage. We entered the flat from the back stairs which led to a fire exit door at the rear of the flat roof. I hadn't decided what to do about Ray. I had no inclination to kill him yet; in the end what happened to Ray would be down to finding the truth. I tied Ray's handcuffs arms to the radiator and his legs from under the table to the radiator after he had been fed watered and had been to the toilet. He didn't like it much but I told him his biggest worry was my not returning if Bella got the better of me.

"Keep your fingers crossed," I said as I closed the door leaving him alone for the rest of the day. As I drove back to Esher the phone rang, it was Winston, I told him to wait a moment whilst I pulled up, I was in the car. I took the next left into a side street, the Road was mainly empty, plenty of spaces to park the car, I pulled up and parked outside a terrace house.

"What have you found for me Winston?"

"Izzy's hit the jackpot my man."

"That's good what has she found?" I wished Winston would stop calling me my man, if anything he was my man, but I had bigger fish to fry and had to let it go.

"I'm all ears Winston."

"Well, first off you were right about Margarita Rodriguez, she came to England twenty four years ago, she was sixteen at the time and after hanging around some pubs and clubs in Newquay she met Chas French the leader of A Paler Shade of Blue, bit of a ladies man is our Mr French so the grape vine tells us. The web site is in Spanish, so you were right to ask someone like Izzy to take on the task."

So far so good I thought.

"What else, Winston."

"That's where it gets really interesting, my man. The web page claims that Margarita was the lead singer with the group, and wrote most of the songs, you can see some hazy 'u tube' recordings with what looks like a tribute band and her singing, but I think they are dubbed with someone dressed up to look like Margarita, she has quite a following in Spain and there is a record label with two albums by Margarita, they sell well apparently. If you asked me I would say the person singing the songs was a sound alike singer and the person on 'u tube' doing the mining was would you believe your housekeeper Bella, we compared some head and eye measurements with the photos you gave me, perfect match. Clever though, the web page goes on to say that Margarita died of pneumonia in the winter of nineteen ninety two in St Ives, she was seventeen and her body was taken back to Madrid where she was buried in the family grave. Looking at the coroners report of her death held in England it states clearly Margarita committed suicide whilst of 'un-sound mind', there's no mention of this on her web page, which goes on to say that another singer Rebecca Davis, nothing *like as good as Margarita* replaced her in the band, this other singer Rebecca was jealous of Margarita and tried to claim she wrote the songs. There is nothing much about Margarita's parents other than they were called Fernandez and Carmen Rodriguez aged forty and forty two at the time of Margarita's death, they live in the suburb of Pueblo Nuevo and Bella's original parents were Sofia and Garcia Lopez they lived in Chamartin north of Madrid, they both died in a car crash. Bella was four at the time and was adopted by Fernandez and Carmen Rodriguez when she was five. Margarita's site is one of the most popular in Madrid, there's even a small shop in the music quarter, Malasama, which sells Margarita's records, CD's, tee shirts and other paraphernalia."

"How did Izzy find our all this in such a short time, Winston?"

"She still has friends in Madrid; it's amazing what you can find my man, if you know where to look." I nodded in agreement.

"Oh, we did find out something about Pedro Rodriguez, from the photo you gave us, Pedro is well known to the police, he's a petty criminal who came originally from Malaga, he worked in bars and night clubs as a bouncer and had been convicted of two counts of GBH before he met Bella. Sounds like a nasty piece of work. There is also a small web site dedicated to Margarita's brother Ernesto who died aged ten. Also we could not find a marriage certificate for Pedro and Bella. Does any of this help you, my man?"

"Yes Winston it's brilliant. What do I owe you?"

"Would five hundred be out of the way my man?"

"No that's fine Winston, its been a big help I'll round it up to seven hundred if you could get down to Esher, meet me at the Bear Hotel in an hour, I have the money for you in Reddies, I'm running short of time."

I called in at the bank, cashed a cheque for seven hundred and got to the Bear ten minutes before Winston, he gave me a typed copy of Izzy's findings, written up as a report, I was impressed, I asked Winston to email the document to my solicitor Teddy Jacob's and thank Izzy for her hard work. I handed Winston the envelope containing the money.

"Thanks my man, good to do business with you."

We shook hands.

"A question for you my man?"

"Go on Winston, ask away."

Why didn't the other members of the group complain when Bella started selling records and claiming Margarita had written and recorded them?"

"That's easy to answer Winston, because three members of the group were implicated in peddling drugs, raping young women and who knows what else, Rebecca and Margarita might just have been the tip of the iceberg."

"Wicked my man."

"You could say that." I watched Winston get in his old Mondeo and pull away into the busy traffic. I had what I needed, worth every penny.

I was half a mile away from home and parked up to ring Bella. She sounded pleased to hear my voice, I said there had been a change of plan and could she drive over to the shops in Esher and buy the best fillet steak for all of us and whatever deserts and wines she would like for her and her parents and Pedro of course. Saying I wanted to celebrate and who better to celebrate with than her and her family.

"That's so nice of you Senor David, I'll go now, mum and dad are watching a film, and Pedro is in the garden. What are we celebrating David?"

"Does there have to be a reason Bella, look we've all been through hell, we are celebrating us, our friendship Bella, you have been so kind and supportive to me since Rebecca's death, I couldn't have managed without you." I tried not to throw up.

"You are such a thoughtful man David, Rebecca was so lucky to have you."

The words were sweet but I detected an edge when she

mentioned Rebecca name, was Bella jealous of a dead person? It seemed like it to me.

Chapter 16

16th February 2017

I hated what I was going to do but it was to be remembered it was me or them. I drove up to my house and parked the Jag up on the carriage drive, then walked over to the workshop; I knew Pedro was in there, I could hear the sound of the lathe. I pushed the door open; Pedro was standing at the lathe turning a piece of apple wood, into a beautiful pear, a finishing chisel in his hand. Beside the lathe were two other Pears, a bunch of Cherries, two Apples and three Plums, that he had turned, they were beautifully turned, no doubt about it. Pedro's turning was first class. I picked up one of the apples.

"Nice apple, Pedro," I said, startling him. When he turned, he looked at me in a pensive manner.

"See Senor." His head was bent down, he wouldn't look at me. I guessed he was unsure what to say or do, I guessed Pedro knew I was for the chop but not when, he turned back to the lathe and carried on with his work. It wasn't his doing, Bella's husband? From what I had learned, I think not, he was I surmised just a hired hand or at best a passenger her handy man and muscle with the same surname. I still had to immobilise him though, as I moved towards him my gun in hand pressed down against my right thigh so he could not see it. But I must have done something to alarm him because he turned again, he had the look and meanness of an angry bull that had just been prodded, this time, head down, his shoulders hunched, he lunged towards me, much faster than before and thrust the chisel towards my chest, luckily the gun came down swiftly on the side of his head before the chisel two inches away from my chest, could do any real damage. I sort of caught him as he fell and half carried, half pushed him down the stone steps in to the cellar, he was that heavy. I checked, he was still breathing, not dead, just stunned, out of breath, I propped him up against a wooden chest which contained some of Rebecca's old clothes, I had intended to give them to a local charity shop, and clambering up the stone steps returned to the workshop, locking the cellar door behind me. I sat for a few minutes, getting my breath back, he was more than one hundred and sixty pounds and the whole short episode had left me exhausted. It was all down to timing, had I been a split second slower, it would have been me in the cellar. I shuddered at the thought of it and then tried to put it out of my mind, there was still work to be done, five minutes past, I had calmed down and was breathing easier still shaken I went to find Bella's parents. Fernandez and Carmen looked harmless enough, sitting in the dining room completing a jigsaw of Windsor Castle, they nodded and smiled as I entered, saying I had something to show them in the study, something I thought they would want to see. They smiled again and slowly getting up followed me in to the study where I had laid out a large map of Spain dated seventeen fifty on my desk which I was sure they would find interesting.

They sat at the desk and looked with interest, whilst I poured them a glass of sherry which I had fortified with several ground down sleeping pills, how strong the potion was, was anyone's guess. They sipped the sherry with Fernandez saying; only the Spanish knew how to make fortified wine. Smiling, I agreed as I watched them peacefully fall asleep. I removed the glasses and locked the study door behind me, now the odds were evens, one against one, just Bella and me. That did not mean it was all over bar the shouting. Bella as I was finding out was very clever and a formidable opponent and wouldn't go down without a fight. I heard the front door open as I came out of the kitchen where I had disposed of the fortified sherry down the sink and washed the glasses, Bella was carrying four shopping bags and a smile as wide as a bus. She was wearing a beige knee length skirt with a split up one side, revealing a sun tanned thigh, a soft brown leather jacket over a white blouse, knee high boots and a small leather shoulder bag, hung over her right shoulder, both the same colour as her jacket, no make up required other than a smidgen of scarlet lip stick on her bow shaped lips, she looked more like a model than a cook/housekeeper, in one word she looked 'sensational' and she knew it. Where did she get the money for those clothes I wondered? I could see she was blissfully happy, as she put the bags down and came over for what I knew would be our first kiss, there was desire and hunger in her eyes, I realised she had waited a long time for this moment. Had I also been waiting too? It was a moot point but I didn't get time to answer. Bella walked up to me and kissed me, rising on tip toe, as if she was Rebecca or my new lover, her small tongue playfully finding mine. I could feel the warmth of her body and the heady smell of her perfume. I nearly lost my balance. I was momentarily intoxicated; Bella finally pulled away and walking into the living room, asked, had I seen Pedro? A guilty conscience or where's my back up? I said unconvincingly, tripping over my words that the last time I had seen Pedro he was in the cellar below the workshop, looking for some wood turning chisels I kept there and without being asked added that her parents Fernandez and Carmen were in the study map reading, a map of Spain I had found for them. She gave me the most curious of looks. It was a silly and un-necessary lie, Pedro was apparently claustrophobic and would never have gone into any cellar alone, something Bella knew but I didn't, I was caught out, sloppy really, I hadn't done my homework, but there you go. There was an awkward moment of silence, then she said smiling as calm as you like.

"You know don't you?" The smile changed to a look of angry defiance on her face as if to say this changes nothing. I could still taste her kiss on my tongue. In a way I was pleased, at least now her involvement was in the open, no more pretending or lies.

"I know some of it Bella, but not all, something I want to ask you how and why you persuaded Rebecca to end her life and why now?"

She walked across the living room and sat down in a beige leather arm chair by the coffee table like she owned it, crossing her legs to show a further expanse of thigh.

"To persuade Rebecca to end her life was relatively easy David, but you would need to be a drug pusher to understand which keys to turn to unlock her mind, to open her up and replace her desire to live with a desire to die." She uncrossed her legs, I tried not to look.

"And you were just helping her along, I suppose?" I knew I had to keep calm and let her talk.

"Yes I used to give her lozenge's to calm her down; they were laced with methadone, easy to purchase over the net, I kept increasing the dose until she became dependant on them and my being with her and then the final push."

I shook my head in disbelief I couldn't believe what she was saying.

"To be truthful David, I enjoyed every minute of it, the power one person has over another, it's like an aphrodisiac." She fixed her eyes on mine; I could feel them boring into me, wondering what she had in store for me.

"And as for the why and when. I knew Ray Guest through a

friend of mine, we exchanged Christmas cards, Ray told me he was once a was a member of the band 'A Paler Shade of Blue' Ray said he was broke and had an idea to blackmail Rebecca also a member of the band, who was very rich, so I said I would help him, for a share of the money and came over to England, Pedro came later."

I tried not to laugh, there was a big lie in what she was saying, no mention of her sister Margarita and her suicide, but I played dumb, nodding as if I believed her every word.

"The blackmail was a joke thanks to Norman Broadbent's stupidity and his side kick the giant Ivan Reberoff, but I had thought of another way to get our hands on Rebecca's money."

I shook my head in disbelief but she was in full swing, so I said nothing and listened.

"Yes, I admit I wanted what Rebecca had, her money, her fine house and most of all you, her husband as my lover." She crossed her legs again, it was a well practiced tactic that was meant to distract me and it was working, I was going to say something and then my mind went blank other than the view of her legs. She was still looking at me intensely, willing me to weaken. I told myself to get a grip, saying.

"The clothes, they are Burberry, how did you come to afford them Bella?"

"I'm glad you asked me that David, it was when I was nursing Rebecca, just before Christmas, she wrote me two cheques, both for four thousand pounds, I hardly had to ask, they were Christmas presents David, it was like taking candy from a child."

"I thought as much," I said, thinking, how could someone be so beautiful and yet so evil. I tried not to show my disgust, I knew she was goading me and it was working, I also realised I hadn't looked at a bank statement in, how long I hadn't a clue. She was still looking at me intently as if the last conversation was of no consequence. I looked at her with equal intensity trying to resist her will and then tried to look away but couldn't; she had that same magnetic allure that Chas French had accept that in her case it didn't matter if the prey was male or female. At that moment, I was the prey, ready in her eyes to be consumed, one way or another. I noticed she had taken her jacket off and it lay on the arm of the chair as she got up and walking towards me and began to undo the buttons of her blouse. I stared for a moment, realising she wasn't wearing anything underneath her blouse, I was mesmerized by the shear beauty of her body; she was like a Spanish flamenco dancer performing on stage.

"What did Ray tell you?" She paused. "I presume you went to see Ray Guest, and not your imaginary friend Malcolm in Brighton?" She spoke confidently, un-afraid, from her point of view, she was in control. I found it impossible to look away from her but managed to say.

"Yes Bella, I saw Ray; he said it was his idea to blackmail Rebecca and when Steve Walker got wind of it Ray arranged through Norman Broadbent to create the gas explosion, as a warning to Steve to mind his own business, but something went dreadfully wrong, Steve and his family were meant to be out watching a film at the local cinema but tragically they were in the house when the timing devise blew the roof off at five to five in the evening, when their son Bobby had been sick in the cinemar, I'm guessing but you came on the scene because your sister Margarita knew Ray some twenty years ago. It was you Bella who saw the big picture, lots of money about five million to be had by all but first you had to get rid of Rebecca. Job successfully completed, I was next in line, but you needed to be sure you could get your hands on the money hence the need for my making a new 'Will' and the creation of the Margarita and Rebecca Foundation. I marvel at your ability to manipulate people so easily." I wasn't going to tell her everything I knew just yet, I wanted her to think I was quite clever but also really stupid and had missed the real reasons for her being here and pushing Rebecca into taking her own life.

"Yes David and we could still put the foundation in place. How clever of you to have worked everything out."

Seemingly satisfied that I knew little of her connection to Margarita. "Ten out of ten," she said, clapping her hands together as her breasts swayed to the movement of he hands, laughing, smiling, she moved a little closer, she was so sure of herself, but I too felt stronger, more confident, but don't ask me why, I knew she would have a gun somewhere on her person, ready to use, if I became difficult.

"Thank you Bella," I said condescendingly, but she didn't notice. "But that's not all is it, there was something else wasn't there, much more important than the money?"

She looked at me for a moment, I thought I saw a tear, but the moisture in her eyes was the shine of defiance.

"It concerns your sister Margarita and her death Bella." I pretended I was probing.

For the first time, she looked away.

"You don't know anything about my sister David."

"I'm afraid you are wrong there Bella, I know your sister Margarita was a small time singer in Madrid, she left your parents home, in Pueblo Nuevo and made her way to England twenty five years ago, she was about the same age as Rebecca, and she auditioned with the band 'A Paler Shade of Blue' at the same time as Rebecca."

"It's not true you can't know that David."

I ignored her outburst, now I had to push my advantage home however painful, I had to go on.

"Don't be silly Bella, there's a website on Facebook, dedicated to your sisters memory, okay, written in Spanish, heavily abridged, leaving out the unpleasant bits that would spoil the image being presented of a brilliant young woman who had tragically been cut down by pneumonia at the age of seventeen, it tells the good parts of her story. There's even a shop in Madrid that you run and is being managed right now by Tomas and Camilla Hernandez, some dedicated friends of yours, keeping the memory of Margarita going and the tills ringing, whilst you are in England, first plotting Rebecca's suicide and now my demise. The embarrassing bits that are missing are that everyone in the band knew, like Rebecca, Margarita had slept with every member of the band other that Ray, his own admission, she even let Norman the roadie have her, but it didn't do her any good, she didn't get to become lead singer of 'A Paler Shade of Blue' as she had hoped, they preferred Rebecca, these facts are conveniently not mentioned on the web site or Facebook."

"Your lying, it's not true." Ignoring her outbursts, I carried on.

"When the members of the band, had had their fill, Margarita, just seventeen, a heroin junkie, pregnant by one of them, penniless and heart broken, took the only exit she thought was available to her, she committed suicide rather than having to go back to Spain and face her parents Fernandez and Carmen, from whom she had stolen their life savings a year earlier to get a boat to France then, Guernsey and finally Cornwall in England, where she made her way to Falmouth, where life was exciting and inviting for a young girl looking for adventure.

"No! No! No! You're wrong David, she died of pneumonia, it was a cruel spiteful winter, Margarita was not used to the cold, wet weather in England."

"I wish that was true Bella, I really do. Nobody deserves to die and in the fashion your sister did, the members of 'A Paler Shade of Blue', apart from Stewart and Rebecca, have in my opinion a lot to answer for."

Her head was bowed, I spoke more gently.

"When things were at their darkest, Bella wrote to you didn't she, telling you what she was going to do and asked for your forgiveness and not to let her parents know the truth, it must have been terrible for you, to have to keep a secrete like that for the next twenty years or so. By the way are Fernandez and Carmen your real parents?" I wanted to play along, though it was getting harder but I had to continue, I still didn't want her to know how much I knew. She looked down.

"No David, they are not my real parents." She gave a sigh. "They adopted me when I was five, my real parents died in a car crash in Madrid, smashed to pieces by a lorry delivering bricks to a building site, the driver Jose Jimenez was drunk, not a scratch on him, he should have died but instead he got life for manslaughter, he served ten years instead of twenty released early for good behaviour. I found out where he lived and spied on him noting when he was at home or out working, I'm proud to say I had my revenge. One night I followed him out of a bar he frequented, he was drunk as usual, I went up to him and told him who I was, at first he couldn't remember, then it dawned on him and he began pleading, begging for his life and saying it was all a tragic mistake, he was crying like a baby when I shot him, he ended up in the bottom of the river Manzanares, near the park, a bullet between his eyes, wearing a body sack. I knew he worked away a lot, sometimes in France and Germany, his wife had divorced him, he was a loner so he wasn't missed and I was never questioned, but to answer your question, yes Fernandez and Carmen were Margarita's parents, there was also a brother Ernesto, but he died aged ten of a brain tumour and now there is just me."

I gave her a compassionate smile, I hated what I was doing but there was no other way, if I didn't want to end up like Jose the lorry driver.

"I believe you came to England Bella to avenge your sister when you learned from Ray Guest how successful Rebecca had been and had remarried and was building a beautiful house."

At first she didn't answer but as she came closer, she allowed the blouse to open fully and at the same time, pulled a small gun from her shoulder bag. I smiled unsurprised by the gun.

"I realised once you had decided to kill Rebecca you needed to know her and my every movement, it was the BT call out when the house was being built a faulty line the BT man said if I remember correctly, I am guessing but he must have planted a bug in the phone which allowed you to listen to every phone call we made, which was how you found out Rebecca was very ill and we needed a house keeper, that's when you sent for Pedro, you were staying with Ray Guest refining your plans, he introduced you to Norman Broadbent who was to be the hit man once my new *will* was in place."

I could see by her face I had struck home, she had been 'found out' but I guessed rightly she was never going to admit to such a wicked plan, she looked a tiny bit ashamed but not enough to put the gun down, she would still kill me if she had to. Putting the pieces together had taken a long time and a lot of luck and help mainly from Winston and his wife Izzy. I realise now, I had kidded myself that I was good at playing detective, in reality I had been a bit of a jerk and missed several opportunities to see the clues and solve the plots against Rebecca and myself. Had I been as good as I thought I was, I would have seen the clues much sooner. Who knows, perhaps if I had been on the ball and a real detective, I could have saved Rebecca. *I'll have to live with that.*

"Put the gun down Bella, you have already caused enough harm." I smiled sympathetically, I suddenly felt tired of playing the game, if she was going to shoot me, I would prefer her to get on with it.

"It doesn't have to be this way David, I would rather you make love to me than I have to kill you, we could be good for each other."

"What about Pedro, your husband?" I asked, still playing dumb, it was a cruel twist in the game we were playing, called life and death, one of us must die. She shrugged, Pedro is Pedro, we have the same Surname that's all, which is convenient, but he's not my husband, he's besotted with me of course and does exactly what I tell him, I thought you would have known that, you're not so clever as you think you are David but no matter, we can get rid of Pedro permanently if you like, its you I want."

"And Norman?" I asked, forcing myself to go on. "Is he for the chop?"

"Yes, silly, silly Norman, he was becoming a real liability, getting mixed up in a turf war and putting my plans at risk. I must say, Pedro excelled himself there, he arranged for Norman to be discharged from Northwick Park Hospital an ugly grey monstrosity of a building, before the police could get their hands on him, and took him for a little ride on the way back to his flat in North Harrow, Pedro took a diversion heading towards Ealing and then Kew Bridge where there was a lot of building development taking place and now Normans part of the foundations of the new car park in Chiswick." Instead of looking ashamed at her handwork, she had regained her composure and smiled, she looked even more beautiful, if that was possible.

"And Ray, what's next in line for Ray then Bella?"

"Ray has a family and a good life style, I don't think he will blab, he's up to his eyes in debt and needs the money more than I do, but like Pedro, he's expendable if he threatened us, I'd snap my castanet's Pedro will kill him and then we will have to kill Pedro." She laughed at her own little joke and gave me an enchanting little smile; she had already decided that we were to be lovers. I didn't know what to say or where to look, her eyes, her face or her breasts, each were working their magic. I settled for her eyes, I needed to know what else she was thinking; my own mind was in turmoil. I wasn't afraid of dying *(so I told myself)*, but I didn't want her to get away with the dreadful things she had done to so many people. *(And yes if I was truthful, I did want to live a little longer.)* I had wondered why she had roped Ray in, now I knew, the penny had finally dropped, Ray was to be the fall guy if anything went wrong, she had promised him fifty- fifty split after paying Norman off to get rid of me. Ray was up to his eyes in debt, I bet he couldn't believe his luck, but it was never going to happen, Bella would have either spilled the beans to the police pointing the finger at Ray as the master mind behind the killings and fraud or Ray would have ended up like Norman as part of the foundations to a new building. Poor old Pedro would be next in line for the chop, then having remortgaged my house and emptied the Margarita foundation of its money she would flit. You had to admire how Bella had thought of everything but I didn't feel sorry for Pedro or Ray. Of course in this scenario Bella had decided like me that things would not work out between us and I was better dead, I would also have been taken to a construction site no doubt by the ever faithful Pedro (*his last task before he joined the list of the disappeared) where* I would be part of the foundations to a new building, the thought of being a part of a building foundation made me feel a little queasy, especially as a new mortuary was being built in Esher. It seems life was cheap to Bella but she had had her share of tragedy, I tried not to show my concern as she came closer, now she was now about four feet away from me, I could breath in the heavy musk, that she extruded, I felt like I could have died at that moment, I was so close to betraying Rebecca, Bella moved confidently to within two feet of me.

"Don't make me fire the gun David." Her eyes were moist, she was holding back tears.

"I'm not making you do anything Bella; I just think things have gone too far, you all but killed Rebecca with the drugs you fed her, in revenge for Margarita's suicide. We both know that, you could never trust me, it wouldn't work." I tried to look calm. "Anyway where did you get the gun, it's a 9mm Largo isn't it. I recognised it from books I had read about the Spanish Civil war. Keep talking, that's what I had read in books, now she was inches away from me, her deep brown eyes pleading with me, her body touching mine. I had two choices, I could embrace her, kiss those sweet lips waiting for me, and surrender myself to her and the Devil or I could try and knock the gun out of her hand and do what was the decent thing to do, incapacitate her until I got hold of the Police or take a bullet if I messed up.

"It was my grandfathers he fought for the Nationalists in the Spanish Civil war, he gave it to my father and my adopted parents gave me a trunk with some of my parents possessions when I was seventeen, I smuggled it into England when I came over by boat, it was easy, no coast guard. It came in useful it was this gun that I used to kill Jose Jimenez, so I know it works perfectly."

Suddenly, just before my time ran out and I had to commit one way or the other, there was a commotion in the hall and the lounge door burst open; I looked round as Prendergast and his assistant Moira came bursting in.

"Put the gun down Bella," Prendergast shouted as he ran across the room, a gun in hand, he was surprisingly nimble for a big man, Moira manned the door her gun pointing towards both of us, if she fired and missed Bella, it was likely I would get hit. Several shots were fired simultaneously, I felt a burning pain in my left shoulder I had been hit. Bella must also have been hit because she fell on to me we ended up on the floor in a tangle. Prendergast was hopping around; shouting and giving orders, it looked like he had been hit in the leg. More police stormed the room, and then everything went deathly quiet. Bella was lifted off me by two burley paramedics; a vacant look from Bella's once beautiful brown eyes told me she was dead. I will never know, what course of action I would have taken, had Prendergast and his body of men had not come in when they did. Would I have surrendered my soul to Bella and the Devil or done the noble thing and tried to play the hero and knocked the gun out of her hand, or taken a bullet if I had been unsuccessful. It was a question which I acknowledged would always be unanswerable. At the time, if I am truthful, I felt deeply ashamed that I could not say with full conviction that I would have done the noble thing. Now I have to carry that question and the only two answers *'yes or no'* around with me, whilst I am still amongst the living. I tried to pull myself up but had to wait until two policemen helped me into a chair. It seemed my injury was not too serious, it was a flesh wound, I was told, more paramedics were on their way.

"Where are Bella's parents?" Prendergast asked.

"Fernandez and Carmen are in the study map reading or more

likely asleep, too much sherry."

"And Pedro?"

"Waking up hopefully in the workshop cellar, by the way Pedro is not Bella's husband, he was her gofer, they just have the same Surname, very convenient."

I handed him the keys to the study and cellar, Prendergast shook his head in bewilderment, and then instructed two men to find them.

"How did you manage to find me?" I asked.

Prendergast sat with his leg propped up on the coffee table and smiled.

"Ray Guest who you kidnapped and kept in your flat in Edgware managed to break one of the windows, a pedestrian alerted the police, you're a very lucky man and I've been shot in the leg for my trouble."

He gave me another half smile.

"Let's get cleaned up here then after we have both been patched up in A&E for our war wounds, you will need to give us a statement. I was going to the match tonight."

I didn't ask him who was playing. Two police officers counselled Bella's parents whilst Pedro asked if they would still be living in the house. Prendergast said there wasn't really enough evidence to tie either of them into Bella's web of deceit, though Pedro would be questioned over his alleged intent to wound when he went for me with the chisel, and Bella's parents would need to provide statements to the police in the morning, so I agreed to pay their hotel bills, whilst arrangements were made for them to return to Spain. One thing was certain; they were not going to spend another night in my house. I needed to be alone. As we opened the front door, Prendergast hobbling out on crutches, me with my arm in a sling, we were stopped in our tracks, the front garden and road outside the house was swarming with reporters. It looked like a circus.

It was the inquest tomorrow which in light of the new evidence would be postponed but all being well they would allow Rebecca's funeral to proceed on Friday.

Bella's parents Fernandez and Carmen along with Pedro were taken in a police car to a nearby hotel near Feltham Police station, they wanted to keep tabs on them, whilst I went with Prendergast to Tolworth Hospital where we had our wounds dressed in A & E and then four hours later we were driven to Feltham police station by Moria Anderson. As we passed Twickenham, Moria said she had an apology to make, I wondered what was coming next.

She said that when they had entered the living room her job was to man the door, when Bella fired at Peter Prendergast, hitting him in the leg she fired at Bella unfortunately missing and hitting me in the shoulder instead. I laughed saying, it could have been worse Detective you might have killed me, and the only saving grace from your point of view would be my not having to make a statement and you could have gone to the match. They both laughed as well out of relief. Who shot Bella, then?" I enquired. Prendergast spoke slowly; I could see he was recalling the incident. "I was very lucky," he said. "We fired at the same time, if Bella had had a split second more time, she would have hit her target, my head or chest and I would have been dead, she knew how to handle a gun, and I'll have the scar to prove it."

We drove on in silence to Feltham Police Station where I attended an extensive interview. It was getting late, but I was keen to get it over with, time hardly mattered to me, Prendergast asked me if I wanted my solicitor present especially as I was likely to be charged with manslaughter and other items including kidnapping. I said I wasn't concerned; I did what I had to do and regretted nothing. To be fair to Prendergast and his assistant Moira Anderson, they were kind and as considerate as they could be. I think they acknowledged, I had taken up the fight but it was not a fight of my making. It was ten thirty when we finished, I was dead beat. I said I would see them for the inquest at the Coroners Court in Woking in the morning. I wasn't Norman Broadbent and wouldn't make a run for it, though poor Norman would not be running anywhere soon, I considered things for a moment and decided it was not my job to inform the police that Norman Broadbent was now part of the foundations of a car park in Chiswick; after all they were the detectives. That quip made Prendergast smile. We shook hands, I took a taxi home and for the first time walked into an empty house, to make matters worse I had run out of whiskey and had to make do with some red wine, 'Merlot' it said on the label, but my knowledge of wine could be summed up in three words, red, white, rose, but it tasted good and initially did the trick, it sent me to sleep.

But I slept fitfully; dreaming of making love to Rebecca's as she was dying in my arms to be replaced by Bella who was in a flaming red and gold flamenco dress she was standing over me. Her black shoes strutting and clacking to the music of 'A darker shade of Blue' her smile at first was inviting and I was pleading for a kiss when she screamed and fell into my arms, there was another woman a girl I couldn't see her face properly, she was singing a song in Spanish walking on the sea shore toward the English Channel, I realised it must be Margarita, I call out her name but she didn't hear me, I shouted again, waving, she was running out to the sea and then Jane looked up and smiled her sweet smile, taking my hand and asking where had I been all this time. I woke up in a sweat and tried desperately to dream the dream again, I needed to see any one of them again, to prove they still alive, I prayed to God that they were and if so, please let me find them. I shut my eyes willing them to appear and the dream to return but I was wide awake and no one was there, I lay on the bed, staring up at the ceiling and named the four women, two I had loved Jane and Rebecca and Bella who under different circumstances I could also have loved and Margarita who I had never met but sensed her pain, they were all dead, my greatest love being Rebecca. I got up drew the curtains and opened the French doors that overlooked the rear garden, a gust of wind caught me unawares, it was four o'clock in the morning, I stared out from the balcony, dawn was breaking, the sky looking angry, wisps of grey cloud scudding across a darker shade of blue. I closed the French doors, drew the curtains back together and went back to bed, I lay back looking up to the blank ceiling again, the house was eerily silent, I realised I was alone other than my ghosts who roamed through the house and my mind at will.

Chapter 17

29th March 2017

Despite my disturbed sleep, I turned up in good time for the inquest at the Coroners Court in Woking Surrey, Teddy Jacob's my solicitor, was furious that I had given the police an interview and write a formal statement without him being present and was now planning to attend the inquest unrepresented. To any normal person I would have sounded completely insane, as I tried to explain to Teddy that I wanted to take my punishment, if the law found me guilty of wrong doing. Teddy did not quite know what to make of my behaviour and excused himself, saying he was only a phone call away if I changed my mind. Something had changed inside me. I would not be moved. Prendergast came over to me and said the coroner was in a funny mood today and I needed to watch what I said, as it happened I was in a funny mood as well. I thanked him for the tip and waited for the inquest to begin. No sooner had it started than Prendergast got up and said new evidence had surfaced in the past twenty four hours and he need time to analyse it as it might be that Rebecca did not simply 'commit suicide', it might have been 'assisted suicide' or even 'murder' Jeremy Fox the Coroner, for some reason looked annoyed when Prendergast began to explain there was new evidence; Fox cut him off and turning to me, saying he wanted to know how and why I had got so deeply involved in what appeared to be police business. I replied that I had completed a detailed description of the events leading up to and on the day of Rebecca's death and other events which followed and how they unfolded in my police statement. I suggested he might want sight of the document.

"Please don't tell me how to conduct my business as the Coroner of this court Mr errs," he looked at his notes, "Mr Rogan."

I countered with my own concerns.

"That was not my intention Sir, but please understand that the only matter of importance to me, is that this inquest determine the exact nature of my wife's death and that you have read my police statement, which would be of assistance to you, which it appears you have not, you can't even remember my name."

Moving his head forward slightly looking at me as if he was peeping over a fence, Jeremy Fox's bifocals fell two inches down from the inset bridge of his rather thin nose, landing on the edge of his nose where they abruptly stopped, perched un- moving on the end of his nose, to show his displeasure. Looking over his glasses he said in a condescending manner.

"Are you represented Mr Rogan?" The bifocal's wobbled slightly but remained perched on his nose, it was a practiced art, pure theatre but it got everybody's attention. He should have been a comedian.

"No," I said definitely, wishing I had some props of my own.

"Then I suggest that when this court reconvenes you are represented by someone who understands the procedures of a coroner's court and can advise his client when to keep his mouth shut."

He adjusted his glasses back into the bridge of his nose, satisfied that he had put me in my place but I was as rattled as him. Reaching for my breast pocket, I pulled out my silk handkerchief; I tied a knot in one end and began waving it around, shouting. "I'll get you, you blighter, if it's the last thing I do."

I looked up at Jeremy Fox whose face was now beetroot red.

With one mighty swipe I shouted. "Gotcha you pesky fly." Stamping my foot on the floor, pretending to kill the fly and replacing my hankie in my pocket saying, "Apologies for that Sir, I detest Blue Bottles, filthy things, I hate the buzzing sound they make, my mother taught me how to swot pesky creatures I didn't like." I looked up giving him the thinnest of smiles, adding, "May I request Sir that when making any reference to my decreased wife I will have no other duty than to correct any statement that is either untrue or demeaning to Rebecca's memory."

I got up and walked out, I knew I had been very foolish but frankly I didn't give a damn.

I was advised later by one of the Ushers that the funeral could precede, the coroner saw no reason to delay although the death certificate had not been issued, it would either be suicide or assisted suicide. It would be a rather sad affair. Plenty of inquisitive people in the congregation but few real friends'. Of course the hearings in the coroner court that involved me were mounting up, in addition to Rebecca's death, there was the death of Ivan Reberoff at my house and also Bella Rodriguez also at my house and the deaths of Stewart Walker and his family. A mighty long list, no wonder the press thought is was hugely funny as well as deadly serious, with, 'deadly' being the apt word amongst the tabloids.

The were having a field day, what they didn't know they made up I was portrayed as a well meaning architect who had lost his pencil at best a hero of sorts but equally stupid and at worst, a very dangerous villain who needed to be locked up, I was probably a bit of all three. Frankly I didn't care what anyone thought, said or wrote, they could all assess my guilt or otherwise between them, I didn't give a fig. I knew I would be going to prison, what for and for how long remained to be established. I realised Prendergast had the decency to wait until after the funeral before formally charging me. The initial charge would I believe be for the manslaughter of Ivan Reberoff. If I was the judge, I would find myself guilty of murder not manslaughter. Alright Ivan was a Russian thug and was looking to kill me but luckily I got in first, two bullets in his buttocks then when he lunged at me, I fired three more shots, the last one I am pretty sure was the one which had killed him, he got me on a bad day, but I used 'excessive force' as they say. Anyway I am glad he's dead, he was and always would have been a thug and a menace to society, if he did go to jail, it would be about eighteen months and out after nine, released for good behaviour by the parole board, he had no place in England, but the truth was I had killed Ivan in cold blood and in the eyes of the law I was a murderer.

Chapter 18
May 2017

The inquest had been put back a week the next event a 'flying circus', for that is what it was becoming was Rebecca's funeral.

Basically there was only Charles Patterson, his wife Betty, Jim Housegood, Jason Hill, Mary Walker, Winston and his wife Izzy and me as the only relation going to attend the funeral, there were a number of colleagues who worked with Rebecca at PPP and that was it.

Though Saint George's Church, Esher was packed out with people, mainly reporters, some standing in the isles and camera crews outside. The Reverend Edward Scott conducted a thoughtful service and gave a meaningful account of Rebecca's short life, saying some kind things about her and marvelling at her voice, he spoke without having to read from notes and sounded genuinely fond of Rebecca and what she had achieved in life. I liked that. There was a wall of tears waiting to be shed, but I managed to hold them back until later when I was alone. I thanked Reverend Scott for taking the service and gave him a cheque for five thousand pounds towards church funds. As we left to attend the interment I noticed an elderly lady sitting on the back pew. She was smartly dressed and I guessed about sixty, I went up to her.

"Excuse me, I'm David Rogan, I was Rebecca's husband, I don't think we have met, are you a friend of Rebecca's or a relation?" The woman looked up and gave me a smile that reminded me of Rebecca.

"I'm Rebecca's aunt Mary Church, my sister Agnes was Rebecca's mother, she was married to Owen Davis, I felt I had to come and pay my respects."

"That's nice of you to be here, are you attending the interment and the refreshment at the Bear Hotel?"

I have just enough time to attend the interment but I have a taxi that will come and pick me up in half an hour and take me to the station. I have two trains to catch before I get back to Colchester where I live."

"Please don't go straight away Ms Church; I can arrange to get you to the station or even drive you to Colchester if we could just talk for half an hour or so." She had a Miss Marple type of face, prim, proper and mischievous.

She stood up and I could see she was thinking.

"Very well Mr Rogan, if you could arrange to get me to Liverpool Street Station for six I can catch a train that will get me in to Colchester around eight o'clock, it's plenty late enough for me."

I proffered my hand, "Please call me David."

We shook hands and made our way to the church grounds, when we arrived at the grave side, the few mourners who were attending this part of the ceremony were waiting for us. I apologised briefly introducing Mary to the handful of people waiting patiently.

When it was our turn to cast earth onto the coffin Mary took a small amount of earth and said, "Good bye Rebecca, God Bless."

As we made our way to the cars we passed minor celebs giving interviews mainly in front of the cameras, saying what a wonderful person Rebecca was and how much they loved her voice, most of them had never met Rebecca but it was good P R. The events were shown on the channel 4 news later in the day along with the BBC and ITV. There was a Skype makeover from Australia with Allen Fender saying how much he loved and missed Rebecca, he looked dishevelled and probably needed exposure to the money swirling around. I wanted to puke but was reminded that this was Rebecca's time to say goodbye, I bit my lip and behaved myself even in front of the television cameras when it was my turn for 'fifteen minutes' of fame or in my case infamy. I wasn't very coherent answering his questions and in the end the interviewer rather embarrassed for both of us, let me go.

A few of us including Mary retired to 'The Bear Hotel where I had hired one of the rooms for refreshments. We took some coffees to an empty table and Mary told me briefly what had happened after Rebecca had run away. She said in those days the title paedophiles was just becoming used for men that behaved in a certain way, she said Owen Davis came into that category and had been arrested for molesting a young girl at school where he worked, six months after Rebecca had run away, somehow he managed to escape from custody and fled out of the country, some people said we ended up in South Africa and others said it was Australia, in any event it took its toll on Agnes and she wasted away and died of pneumonia early in February the following year.

"And what about you, what have you been doing?" I asked.

"Not much, I never married, I worked for the inland revenue and they retired me when I was sixty, I have tried to get a job ever since but I am usually told I am too old."

I thought for a moment, have you heard that we are planning on creating a foundation in Rebecca's name for young musicians."

"Yes I read it somewhere, nice idea."

Well its early days but the foundation will need someone to run it and also deal with the mountain of letters which have been sent to Rebecca, having a member of her family run the foundation would be excellent, would you consider it Mary?"

She looked at me thoughtfully again. It's a nice idea David, but I live in Colchester."

"Well come and live here with me, I have a huge house which was Rebecca's, have a trial period keeping the house you have in Colchester and if it doesn't work out," she cut me short, "this is all happening too quickly David, I need time to think?"

"Have all the time you want but please say yes," adding, "nothing ventured, nothing gained." She smiled; I don't think she was used to someone having the last word.

I handed her my card and said if she was ready I would drive her to the house for a brief look and then take her to Colchester. She asked if it wasn't too far, I said, "No, I could do with a drive." I realised I hadn't spoken to the handful of guests presents and made light of this by saying I had just had the pleasure of meeting Rebecca's aunt who might consider running the foundation for us. Charlie and Betty came over and having introduced themselves said that they knew Rebecca through PPP and were to be trustees of the foundation and would be happy to provide help and support if needed. I could see it was all a little too much for Mary and thankfully the refreshments did not last long. Its difficult to make meaningful conversation when someone you love or who you know has committed suicide. Afterwards we drove straight to the house, which was a couple of miles down the road, Mary took in a beep breath when she saw how large the house was and the reporters five deep on the road. I spent half an hour or so showing Mary the house, I could tell she felt comfortable, she said she could feel Rebecca's presence in the house and that she liked the housekeepers living quarters, it was nice and private. I took that as a good sign, we left at half five and I made my way anti clockwise on the M25 and then the A12 to Colchester, it was a long drive, close to one hundred door to door, but I was enjoying Mary's company, she told me stories of how she and Agnes played together as children, though she was five years younger than her sister, she didn't live in a house but in a small retirement bungalow, I could see she was tired and did not keep her, she promised to think about what I had suggested and said she would be in touch.

I got home at eleven, I must have consumed about three quarters of a bottle of whiskey before I slowly climbed the stairs on all fours and unable to haul myself on to the bed, fell in to a deep sleep on the floor the best sleep I had had in weeks, thankfully the sleep was dream free.

I woke next morning to the sound of knocking on the door. I went down in my dishevelled clothes and uncombed hair and, on opening the door was charged with the manslaughter of Ivan Reberoff by Peter Prendergast. I nodded and asked if he would come in a moment so I could change before he took me to Feltham Police station. Prendergast nodded back and followed me to my bedroom.

I changed quickly, combed my hair and brushed my teeth, and then we walked back down the stairs and to the waiting police car. There were cries and questions from reporters in every direction but I heard only the crescendo of noise.

I was glad to be leaving for a while, I hadn't realised how tired I was. When I was taken into custody care of H M Prison Coldingly, Bisely, Surrey, I did not protest or request bail. In jail I was mainly ignored by my fellow in-mates, I had been charged with the manslaughter of a Russian giant, so in their eyes I was capable of violence and murder, which meant I was unpredictable and best left well alone, Equally the wardens didn't quite know what to make of me I came over as cultured but was also considered a villain.

A few days later I was charged with GBH by Prendergast for the injuries to Norman Broadbent, a broken leg. Herman Cain the beef cake, three broken ribs and Kurt Geiger who I had named Mr Tattoo, two broken legs and broken pelvis sounded painful. I made no plea.

I was allowed to attend Rebecca's inquest which gave a verdict of assisted suicide. They got something nearly right, I guess Rebecca's letter clinched it in terms of proof for Fox, but I knew Rebecca would never have gone that far without Bella's help, so much for Jeremy Fox should have gone to 'Spec Savers.'

A few days later Jeremy Fox the Coroner came to a different the verdict for the death of Ivan Reberoff, Unlawful killing, that put me in my place.

I learned through the prison grapevine that they had found lawful killing of Bella Rodriguez.

The Coroners court in Salisbury were unable to come up with a verdict for poor Stewart Walker and his family. A date was set for my trial, at the pre trial; I insisted I remain unrepresented and got told off by the judge for refusing to give a plea. I enjoyed that, stuff the lot of them, I gave him a stony stare.

Chapter 19
June 2017

The trial regarding the death of Ivan Reberoff held at Kingston on Thames Crown Court was a bit of a farce right from the start. First Norman Broadbent his alleged employer and the prosecutions chief witness, had disappeared off the face of the earth. I knew from Bella's confession, that poor Norman was now part of the new 'Chiswick Car Park' foundations; I didn't consider it my place to inform the prosecution service. Second, the only real evidence the prosecution had was my statement which I had given the police. I stated that Ivan Reberoff had entered the rear garden of my house and was trying to gain access via the first floor bedroom. In my police statement, I had said.

Had Ivan Reberoff been on lawful business he would have knocked on the front door during daylight hours, not at two thirty in the morning. I had then gone on to say, when challenged Reberoff fired three shots at me which all missed, *(this was not quite the truth)* I returned the fire, two shots in his buttocks and then three more, when he came charging at me like a wild animal, having fallen from the roof. It was established at the post mortem that it was the last bullet from my gun which had killed him. Also in my statement there was the reference to the fact that Ivan Reberoff had threatened to kill me after the abortive blackmail of Rebecca Davis my girl friend at the time, some months earlier. Every one including the jury, could tell that the judge was not amused by the total lack of evidence against me presented by the prosecution, and made less helpful by my refusal to enter a plea or give evidence in my defence upon which I could be cross examined by the prosecution council, even if it was my right.In the end the judge had no alternative than to have the case thrown out and gave a serious reprimand to the prosecution council and the CPS for a lack of evidence.

Of course I wasn't free; I was still on remand in Coldingly Prison for the GBH charges against Norman Broadbent and his two cohorts.

With Norman dead and Herman Cain the beef cake and Kurt Geiger, both having done a runner, of course neither could run anywhere after their injuries, so let's assume they disappeared with someone's help. The case against me was likely to go the same way. The press had another field day. For some reason there was much clapping shouting and banging when I was returned to prison, I went to my cell and kept myself to myself.

The trial charging me with GBH was to take place in a week's time, again at Kingston Crown Court. On the actual day of the trial; there was much concern in the prosecution camp. With ten minutes left before the trial was to commence there was no sign of Norman or his two henchmen, Herman Cain or Kurt Geiger.

As before I was asked to submit a plea which I declined much to the judge's irritation and I was threatened with contempt of court when I laughed at the judge and gave him a salute. I shrugged they couldn't send me to jail because I was already there. A point not lost on the judge. There was a very hostile press outside, I was referred to, as David as in David and Goliath, Goliath being a multi headed giant, comprising the police, the prosecution service and the judge. Had I had a catapult like David had in the bible story I would have aimed my stone at the judges head hopefully dislodging his wig, like a lot of people in authority he was a prig. Of course I was flattered by the attention, but I knew it wouldn't stop them sending me to jail, neither did I care much, the love of my life, Rebecca had been driven to suicide by perhaps the coldest person I was ever to meet for money, power and revenge. The truth was that since Rebecca's death I had turned into a criminal, no better than Norman Broadbent. In fact much worse, I didn't quite feel shame or guilt if I felt anything it was numbness. I was still reeling from the events of the past six months. Charlie came to visit me a few times and said he would arrange for the house to be looked after if as most people believed I would be sent to jail, the most likely outcome of the trial. But this was a case of lightening striking twice; the charges of GBH were thrown out due to key witnesses not turning up to give evidence, as before there wasn't any other evidence other than hearsay, and my statement given to the police on my arrest.

The judge said in his summing up, it gave him no pleasure to have the case thrown out and my impending release from jail, and to his mind I was of dubious character at best and potentially a serious villain. He wore plastic rimmed glasses similar to Jeremy Fox the coroner but he didn't have Jeremy's dexterity to make them drop from bridge of his nose to the tip of it, for one reason he had a crimson red drinkers chubby snub nose about three quarters of an inch long and large rubbery red lips and a white goatee beard, he reminded me of a garden gnome.

I had not spoken at either trial and following the judge's remarks I challenged him to repeat the remarks outside of court in front of the press.

There was a look of rage on his face as he turned and walked out of the court.

No one spoke to me; I was lead away to go back to the remand prison where I would be formally released. Charlie sent his chauffeur to pick me up upon my release and drove me home when I got home I noticed that he had stocked the fridge and freezer with food and most important a fillet steak and two bottles of my favourite scotch and a note from Charlie saying, 'don't be a stranger, David'.

I was really touched by his gifts and once I had got settled I would phone and thank him. I had a good old soak in the bath accompanied by the scotch and read some of the mail which had piled up. Nothing of real interest other than one letter from Mary Church it was five days old. I sat in the bath and read it.

Dear David

I have given a lot of thought to your suggestion of my undertaking the running of the 'Rebecca Davis-Rogan Foundation' of course, once you explained what it was and that it was to be in Rebecca's family name, I don't think I had much choice, so if you can agree to some simple requests I would be delighted to give it a go, its an opportunity for me to do something purposeful with the rest of my life. These are my red lines.

1. *I have spoken to the council regarding the renting of my flat and they are prepared to allow me to live elsewhere for three months provided the rent and rates are paid and the property is properly alarmed and kept in good order. I do not anticipate that things won't work out but this is a good safeguard for both of us. Would you pay these expenses please?*
2. *I presume we will be working from one of the reception rooms, which is fine by me, to clear the mountain of letters already delivered and sat on your dining room table I would like the assistance of one or two young women to help me with replying to the letters and setting things up. They of course will need to be*

paid. Given that I will be living rent free and food etc. provided I will only need a modest salary say five thousand pounds per year.

3 *I would like to live in the small housekeepers flat if that is agreeable to you, I realise it was occupied by Bella Rodriguez but it would suit me and also give each other space, perhaps it could have a coat of paint and my furniture brought over.*

4 *I have a cousin Jennifer who comes to visit me usually for two weeks in August and sometimes at Christmas, I would like to feel she could come and stay with me in Esher.*

5 *I may need to go to college or somewhere like to understand fully what my duties are for running the foundation, will the foundation cover these costs.*

6 *I don't drive but would like the opportunity of learning to drive if you could assist with the cost of the lessons and provide me with a small car if I can master driving.*

That's about it, if you are agreeable to the items above you can come and collect me and my stuff that I gathered over a period of sixty years and will need radical pruning, and as they say in America, I'm good to go.

Kind Regards Mary Anne Church

The scotch went down well and after drying off, I rang Mary and apologised for not replying sooner and said today's Wednesday how about I come over on Saturday, give us the weekend for her to settle in. I also said I would contact my solicitor Teddy Jacob's who would draw up a draft agreement for us to agree which would cover the points raised and launch the Foundation in a formal manner and duty holders appointed. She sounded as excited as I was; it was for both of us a great way to live with the memory of Rebecca. I went to bed which compared to the bed in my cell was like being in heaven.

I slept for twelve hours solid. When I looked out of the window the street was still full of reporters. I showered, dressed in jeans and a long sleeve jumper, combed my hair and brushed my teeth and went down to face the press.

When I opened the door I was greeted by a barrage of questions I held my hand up and after a minute or so they quietened down. As per usual I thanked them for being patient and said I understood they had a job to do.

They began firing off questions and I held my hand up again saying you must realise I am very tired and would be pleased if say twenty of them came back tomorrow morning when they would be invited into the house and I would answer around twelve to fifteen questions over a cup of tea or coffee and a bun.

For a moment they all looked puzzled, there must have been fifty to a hundred reporters in the garden and road.

"Well you will just have to draw lots but number twenty one will be Johnny Haynes from the local paper, 'The Surrey Comet'."

I could see the delight on Johnny Hayes face. It was a bit of a scoop for him and anyway if they were going to write about me I wanted the locals to hear what I believe actually happened. I phoned the local bakery in town and they readily agreed to provide tea and coffee for twenty five guests with bacon and sausage sandwiches and cheese for vegetarians. I offered then a further one hundred and fifty pounds if I could borrow Jill for a couple of hours, to help with the catering, when the reporters turned up. They agreed readily it was a weight off my mind. I liked the idea of entertaining the press it also gave me a degree of control, I also decided to prepare a written hand out which would cover most of the questions I thought would be raised, it gave me the opportunity of answering the question in a way that suited me and the answers were on record restricting their ability to change the emphasis or wording of my replies. By the time I had finished and printed off the screed, I was half way down the second bottle of Scorch but I didn't care, I felt good and relaxed for the first time since Rebecca became unwell. I made sure I was up early. Jill Canning arrived at nine thirty with the food and drink and we were on our way, I had opened the doors between the lounge and dining room and placed twenty one chairs in a semi circular pattern, having to borrow four from Bella's flat It felt strange being there, I could still feel her presence. I would have to arrange for her furniture and crockery, personal belongings and clothes to be shipped back to her parents in Spain.

The reporters started to arrive at ten fifteen and ten twenty and by ten thirty we were ready to rock and roll, each reporters was handed my screed along with a sandwich and a drink by Jill.

I could see a glum look on some of their faces as I had second guessed some of the questions they were going to ask, what a shame.

The exchange of questions was reasonably good natured and polite.

I think most of those present realised I had taken a physical and emotional battering over the past months, what they were most interested in was Bella's relationship first with Rebecca and then myself.

The juicy stuff.

This information was on my screed and I told them, what Bella said when she found out, I knew she was somehow involved in

Rebecca's death and was plotting mine.

There was a palpable silence when I spoke, I went on to say that as well as wanting to kill me but she would have preferred to have kept me for herself With Bella it was one or the other, and on the fateful day she died I was ashamed to admit at gun point, I could have succumbed to her wishes, I hadn't but I could have. She had a power that was frightening, several reporters nodded in recognition that they might have done the same if they were in similar circumstances, which pleased me. One of the reporters asked me if I knew that Chas French had fled from St Ives across the English Channel to France where it was thought he had made his way to Spain, it is believed he is either hiding in Gibraltar, Northern Spain or Portugal. Abandoning his young wife Sissy and their child. I said no I wasn't aware of that but it did not surprise me. The same reporter then said that Ray Guest had also picked up sticks and left his house in Ham Common which had been remortgaged up to the hilt, he had also emptied his bank account and fled, it was believed to be Thailand. His wife Jenny and two children had been left homeless with the repossession of the house pending and were now living with her mother in Richmond. No, I said I didn't know that either, but again it didn't surprise me. I was then asked if I regretted any of my actions. I said no, the only regret was not finishing off Chas French when I had the opportunity but I had other things to focus on and realised bringing Chas French and Ray Guest to face the charges against them was a police matter and I wanted to thank Detective Inspector Peter Prendergast and Detective Moria Anderson for the way they had treated me during a very difficult time. I guess I was trying to put the record book on my behaviour straight. Another reporter asked where Bella was to be buried. I said I had made arrangements for her to be taken by plane to Spain, I didn't mention the cost, which I considered extravagant but looked at with a compassionate eye. Bella had not been dealt the best of cards, it must have been very difficult to live with losing her parents at the age of four, being adopted then the suicide of her sister Margarita and her brother Ernesto also dying at the age of ten, it was not surprising in some ways, she went off the rails. The final question was the most relevant, where did I go from here? I said in truth I had no idea. Two months ago I didn't care if I lived or died, but I am very pleased to have discovered the truth behind Rebecca death, I never believed it was just suicide, Rebecca was stronger than that. Now I want to do something useful with the rest of my life and with the Royalties from Rebecca's songs I wanted to create a foundation for young musicians and Mary Church, Rebecca's aunt had agreed to run the foundation, Charlie Patterson and his wife Betty were to be appointed as trustees, and Teddy Jacob's my solicitor had kindly offered his services as the Trusts secretary. It was good to have something positive to think about.

The reporters left at twelve o'clock, I saw them out and then I rang Charlie to thank him for his kindness and invited him and Betty out for a meal.

"Yes," he said. "But slight change of plan."

"Come to us tomorrow seven thirty for eight, David we're having a dinner party and we are one short, a man as it happens." I could hear him laughing and Betty his wife telling him off for being so rude in the background.

"I know you have had no luck with blonds and brunets David." I could tell we was enjoying himself and ignoring Betty telling him to have some decorum.

"You'll be sitting next to Susannah Burns, she's a well known Scottish sculptress, interesting name, don't you think?"

I heard Betty say. "Really Charles, the mans still in mourning."

"Be quiet Betty I'm on the phone, and by the way David she's a red head, ha ha."

He had done it again, got me out of myself, I was laughing as well, and thinking there's hope for the wicked.

"I'll need to press my DJ Charles."

"Good man," he said.

All that was left was to get through the dinner un-scathed with my partner for the evening, Susannah Burns and drive over to Colchester Saturday morning, where I would be meeting Winston who had hired a removal lorry and bring Mary Church back to her new home in Esher.

About the Author

I was a 'war baby'. My mother, Nora Donnelly, had a brief romance with Donald Ettinger, 'an American GI'. I was born in a private nursing home in a place called East Sheen close to Kew Gardens on the 1st of September 1944. The name on my birth certificate read Michael Roy Donnelly, father unknown. Sometime in 1944, my father was posted to Europe and in 1945, returned to America, not England to my mother's surprise. I grew up not knowing my father; it is fair to say that he may not have known of my existence. I was known as Michael Ettinger at Kindergarten, and my name was formally changed by deed poll to Michael Roy Donnelly Ettinger to coincide with a second baptism and first communion when I was seven years old. Unsurprisingly, I was an immature and shy child.

My saving grace, after a short spell in a foster home, was that my Grandmother brought me up whilst my mother, who lived with us went to work. I used to call my grandmother, Mum. It was not until I was nineteen and ready to marry that my Uncle Ted told me that Nora was my birth mother. Funnily, she had also changed her name from Donnelly to Ettinger. When I was about 12, though, she never told me why. In many ways, none of this mattered, though I never liked having to explain about my father when asked. But like everyone else, I got on with my life. It was only much later, at the age of 64, it was an email sent on the spur of the moment through cyberspace from a man I had never met in St George, Utah that everything changed.

Unbelievably, I had traced my father and discovered that I had three brothers and two sisters. Alas, I was unable to meet Abby, the older sister who had died. My father, Donald Ettinger, known in the American football annuals as **'Red Dog'**, had come into my life. But like Abby, he had died before I was able to meet him. He was very much alive to me, so too were my three wonderful brothers and surviving sister who treated me like I had always been part of their family, 'a story in itself'.

Ever since I can remember, I had yearned to visit America, to become an **'American Citizen'**. I always felt American; it was my birthright, something that had been denied as I lived my life in England. It wasn't that I was unhappy. It was just that something had always been missing, an empty space inside of me waiting to be filled. The irony of my mother changing my name from Donnelly to Ettinger was that it became the key to finding my family in America. The icing on the cake was being granted American Citizenship some 18 months later. I love England and Yorkshire, where I live with my wife Angela; I am proud to be British, but my heart and soul belong to America. Eight short years ago, unplanned, a dream came true. Now I feel I belong. I have found my roots, the love of my brothers and sister and have an American identity. It is a wonderful feeling that words can never properly describe.

Why bother to write
when you get as lucky as this, you might ask:

As a child, my Grandmother used to read to me. What a luxury that was, snuggled up to her by the coal fire, her gentle voice bringing to life the characters in Dickens' novels from which I never tired. It was the foundation of my fascination with books and reading, the perfect companion for a solitary child. I can't speak for those children who have brothers and sisters. I have only had mine four years but reading suited me as a child and still does.

Art, in any form, be it a novel, a painting, a film, a song or piece of music can be likened to a bus, a plane, a car or train. They are vehicles that transport us to someplace else, where free from our daily routines and responsibilities, we enjoy 'an interlude' in our lives. We enter another world to dream, fantasize and share the lives of people and places, real or imaginary.

The beauty of books is that you can take them anywhere, pick them up, put them down, read and re-read them at will. For many people, a book becomes a friend, a companion like a favourite record, a painting, a poem or a film that is always there. Books are timeless but immediately accessible that we can take with us through life, dipping in and out of our favourite books from time to time, an indulgence of endless pleasure.

My aim in writing is to write something that makes the reader smile and maybe laugh. There are plenty of writers out there that provide shock and awe. Luckily, there is enough room for all of us. I prefer to evoke the feel-good factor. Perhaps, you might say, "this is a little sentimental". Okay, I hear you. But, isn't that what we all want at various times in our lives, something to read that feels good, that's a little predictable, that doesn't hurt or impinge? Other than for my own pleasure, that is why I write.

Other Books
by Michael Ettinger

Lens Notes
published by Michael Terence Publishing, 2020

Len's Notes chronicles the last year of his short life as told by Henry Red Feather a Native American Indian who was his friend and shared a flat with him in Egypt.

Len was a young Egyptian mathematician whose brilliant mind bordered on that of a genius but was equally fragile. He died of a brain haemorrhage at the age of 26 leaving behind many notes, mathematical papers and unfinished theories as to whether the universe and mankind were a product of natural evolution or the creation of God. His other great quest was to find a value for zero.

Len's notes also challenge many scientific claims that are mainly computer-driven, based on clever simulation presented as fact, but in reality are no more than theoretical and can never be substantiated in a way that can be readily understood by society.

Following his death, Len's father asked Henry to assemble his son's notes into a book. The notes capture the drama, elation of new discoveries, the lows of depression and the curse of self-doubt. Entwined within Len's notes are Henry's recollections of his own life. Len's notes provide new insights into the questions Paul Gauguin asked in his famous painting, 'Where did we come from, why are we here, where are we going'.

Three Murders, One Body
published by Michael Terence Publishing, 2020

Awaiting publication:

Trudy

Must Have Poems

White Wash

The sleepy, gated village of Baniston, 12 miles north of Stevenage, comes to life when two people are found dead within days of each other.

Peter Thompson, the owner of the estate, is concerned more about the effect the incidents will have on the village and his vast income than on the unfortunate deaths.

Audrey Mosley, the village vamp, whose tennis coach gave her after match "lessons" worries about what might come out of the woodwork. While husband, Richard, seems unable to come to terms with his wife's infidelity. To add to his woes, he also suffered the loss of his beloved show tomato plants which were destroyed before the village fete.

Clive Johnson, deep into plumbing, and his wife, Janice, along with Tina, the hairdresser, disgruntled Tom Grangemore who used to work for Richard Mosley, Ben Griffin retired farmer and ex lightweight boxer together with Inspector Peter Prendergast and his team of detectives bring colour and amusement to this fast-moving and thoroughly enjoyable read.

Smile and laugh through this spoof murder mystery.

Available worldwide from Amazon
and all good bookstores

---

www.mtp.agency

www.facebook.com/mtp.agency

@mtp_agency

Ingram Content Group UK Ltd.
Milton Keynes UK
UKHW011002170323
418727UK00002B/408

9 781800 945128